"Do I make you hot?"

Zac slid his hands up and down her upper arms, the rhythmic contact depriving her of all rational thought and possible responses as he gazed at her with hunger and greed and passion.

"I don't know what to say—"

"You have no idea what you do to me when you look at me like that."

He tugged her close a second before crushing her lips beneath his. The scorching kiss, a sensual assault, left her reeling.

As she tilted along with the deck beneath her shaky feet, she realized she'd never been kissed like this—ever.

She clung to him as his lips teased her to match him. She moaned, a guttural sound deep in her throat, and the noise inflamed him as he leaned into her, pressing her back against the rail and setting her wildest desires alight.

She should stop this madness, re-erect the barriers that had come crashing down the first instant his lips had touched hers.

But it felt so good to be desired, so good to have the attention of a man, so good to obliterate any lingering memories of what had happened on this night over three years ago....

What do you look for in a guy? Charisma. Sex appeal. Confidence. A body to die for. Looks that stand out from the crowd. Well, look no further—the heroes in this miniseries have all this, and more! And now that they've met the women in these novels, there is one thing on everyone's mind....

NIGHTS *of* PASSION

One night is never enough!

These guys know what they want and how they're going to get it!

Don't miss any of these hot stories, where romance and sizzling passion are guaranteed!

Nicola Marsh

TWO WEEKS IN THE MAGNATE'S BED

NIGHTS *of* PASSION

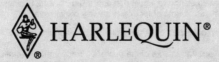

HARLEQUIN®

TORONTO • NEW YORK • LONDON
AMSTERDAM • PARIS • SYDNEY • HAMBURG
STOCKHOLM • ATHENS • TOKYO • MILAN • MADRID
PRAGUE • WARSAW • BUDAPEST • AUCKLAND

Recycling programs
for this product may
not exist in your area.

ISBN-13: 978-0-373-12858-7

TWO WEEKS IN THE MAGNATE'S BED

First North American Publication 2009.

All about the author...
Nicola Marsh

NICOLA MARSH has always had a passion for writing and reading. As a youngster, she devoured books when she should have been sleeping, and later she kept a diary, which could be an epic in itself! These days, when she's not enjoying life with her husband and son in her home city of Melbourne, she's at her computer doing her dream job: creating the romances she loves. Visit Nicola's Web site at www.nicolamarsh.com for the latest news of her books.

Nicola also writes for the Harlequin® Romance line.

With thanks to fellow Harlequin Romance
author Claire Baxter, for helping me brainstorm
Zac in all his dynamic, enigmatic glory!

CHAPTER ONE

As THE taxi screeched to a halt, Lana Walker flung open the door and scrambled for her bags.

'Hey, slow down. You haven't missed the boat.'

The deep groove in the driver's caterpillar mono-brow had been honed with years of practice if his glare was any indication.

The way she saw it, she might have arrived on time to board the *Ocean Queen*, but she'd missed the boat metaphorically in every other way that counted—which was exactly why she was taking this trip.

She rummaged for the fare and darted a curious glance at the ship, spotting several officers in white uniforms on deck.

Very impressive—and the ship wasn't half bad either.

A shadow loomed over the open passenger door as the driver held out his hand. 'Some people have all the luck. How about my fare, lady?'

Grouch. She resisted the urge to poke out her tongue as she handed him the money, picked up her luggage and headed for the escalators.

What would he know about luck? She'd worked hard for what she had—damn hard: five years as curator at Melbourne

Museum, and three years as head curator at Sydney Museum had been amazing, stimulating and stressful.

Sure, she had a stellar reputation in the industry, and a gorgeous apartment in the beachside suburb of Coogee, but that was about it.

She didn't have a life.

No time out, no socialising, no fun.

Over the next two weeks she planned to change all that.

Though luck had played a part in this trip; if she hadn't won the cruise she wouldn't have taken a holiday, sad workaholic that she was.

As thoughts of work crowded her head, namely how she'd recently missed out on the opportunity of a lifetime courtesy of her crippling shyness, she stumbled at the top of the escalator and pitched forward, silently cursing the three-inch heels her shoe-crazy cousin Beth had loaned her for the trip.

So much for the hope that the illusion of height would give her extra poise. It would be difficult to feign elegance when she landed on her butt.

Grabbing wildly at anything more stable than air, she exhaled on a relieved sigh as a strong pair of arms shot out, holding her in a vice-like grip.

'Whoa. These things are lethal if you don't concentrate. Too busy daydreaming about the *Love Boat,* huh?' The smooth voice, with more than a hint of amusement in its husky depths, sent an unexpected shiver down her spine as she looked up into her rescuer's face.

Wow.

Seeing good-looking guys on a daily basis was a perk of her job. The museum was a haven for sexily scruffy archaeological students, attractive teachers, even the odd university professor with a distinguished Sean Connery thing going on.

Yet this guy who now pinned her with arms displaying a great set of biceps was so much more than that. Striking was more appropriate. Even sex-on-legs, as brazen Beth would say.

Hypnotic eyes, a deep, cobalt blue, were fringed with long dark lashes any woman would have envied, and those baby blues were pinned on her, a teasing glint in their rich depths.

She inhaled sharply, unprepared for an intoxicating fresh citrus scent that left her head spinning—and not just from her near-fall.

As for his lips, curving with the hint of a smile, for the first time in her reclusive life she understood the label 'kissable'.

All too aware she was staring—gawking, more like it—she dropped her gaze. Only to be confronted by an equally intriguing sight: a broad expanse of tanned chest where the two top buttons of his shirt were undone.

Hotter than Indiana Jones, leapt to mind.

She had a major thing for Indiana—always had—and, lucky her, Indiana's double was holding on to her as if his life depended on it.

She'd wanted to gain confidence, step outside her comfort zone, experience new things on this cruise. To broaden her outlook to the extent she was never passed over for a work opportunity again. She had been thinking along the lines of dance lessons, lectures on exotic destinations, shore excursions, that sort of thing.

However, being held by this guy had her mind sailing down channels she'd never usually contemplate. Not a bad thing entirely, if taking this holiday had already affected her mindset. Maybe shy, geeky Lana—as she'd once overheard some colleagues call her—was already slipping into vacation mode.

Her heart thumping, whether in fear of her strangely errant thoughts or excitement at what they might urge her to do, she eased out of his grip.

He grinned and, typically, he had a sexy smile to match the rest of him. 'So, do I pass inspection?'

Great. He knew she'd been checking him out. Her skill at covert observation was on a par with her wardrobe: shabby at best.

'What makes you think I was inspecting anything? You were holding me so tight I had nowhere to move, let alone look.'

'Feisty. I like that.' His eyes gleamed, and the corners of his too-tempting-for-comfort mouth twitched in amusement.

Heat suffused her cheeks as she struggled to come up with a comeback. She hated how she always thought of a great retort ten minutes too late.

How was it she could answer any student's query in a second, but right now her brain—a whiz at cataloguing priceless artefacts, leading tour groups and calculating storage data—was totally befuddled?

'Thanks for breaking my fall.'

As replies went, it was pretty lame. Pathetic, in fact; it looked as if her comeback skills had sunk to the same level as her flirting expertise: below average bordering on non-existent.

More embarrassed than she cared to admit, she managed a tight smile, picked up her luggage and turned away, striding towards the ship though her knees wobbled like just-set jelly.

'Watch your step!' he called after her, his voice shaking with laughter.

She stiffened, but didn't break stride, determined not to look back, refusing to give him the satisfaction. Besides, she could feel his stare boring holes into her back.

Her skin prickled at the recollection of those incredibly blue eyes twinkling at her, laughing at her, and she shook her head in disgust. She was such a novice at this.

'Live a little, cuz. Let your hair down. Go crazy,' Beth had encouraged her. 'You've got two weeks to cut loose, to be someone you wouldn't dream of being on land. Make the most of it.'

Great advice, and it had sounded easy coming from her bubbly, confident cousin, who bounced through life with a perpetual smile on her face. And Beth sure knew what she was talking about, considering her positive attitude had landed her Aidan Voss, the dreamiest husband on the planet.

As for Beth's other advice—'dust off the cobwebs, get laid'—Lana blushed just thinking about it.

It was precisely three years, two months and five days since she'd last had sex. Not that she was counting or anything. Besides, she'd have to date to have sex—would have to get emotionally involved with the guy to contemplate it—and she didn't trust her emotions any more; not after what Jax the Jackass had done.

She tucked her old holdall under her arm tighter and headed for the gangway. Beth was right. While her professional life shone, her social life sucked. She had no confidence, no social skills, and no hope of being chosen for the museum's next overseas jaunt unless she learned to be more assertive, more outgoing, more *everything*.

Maybe this cruise would be just what a conservative curator needed?

Zac watched the petite brunette cut a path through the crowd, confused and intrigued.

Most of the holidaymakers he met were dressed to kill, and wearing enough make-up to sink a ship—no pun intended—yet she wore a simple navy suit bordering on severe, and barely a slick of lipgloss. And yet she had managed to capture his attention anyway.

He'd reached out to her in an instinctive reaction, but once she was in his arms his synapses had short-circuited and he'd found himself wanting to hold on way longer than necessary.

What was with that?

He'd lost any tender regard towards the fairer sex around the time Magda had done her chameleon act, and he hadn't let a woman get close enough to sink her talons in since.

Unwittingly, his gaze was drawn to the diminutive figure striding towards the ship, head up, shoulders squared, as if ready for battle. No simple walking for her. No, sirree. She had to sway her hips in a natural, tantalising rhythm in sync with her legs.

Running a hand across his eyes didn't help his quest to wipe her imprint from his retinas. Her sexy gait was replaced by an instant image of feline hazel eyes and a full, pouting mouth. Lord, that mouth. He could fantasise about it for ever. As for that innocent schoolgirl-channelling-schoolmarm expression she had down pat—he'd never seen anything like it.

When she'd stared at him with those striking burnt caramel eyes she'd appeared wide-eyed and ingenuous one second, and ready to give him a severe scolding the next.

Interesting. Very interesting. But he didn't have the time or the inclination to follow up on the first woman to pique his interest in a long time.

He had more important things on his mind—like doing a damn good job the next two weeks before he moved on to the next stage of his life. His uncle wanted him here. They'd noticed a pattern to the series of accidents that had plagued their cruise fleet, and the pattern suggested that the *Ocean Queen* was the next target. He planned for it to be the last.

After unpacking, Lana made her way to the promenade deck and wandered away from the crowds along the railings, finding a deserted spot with a clear view of the hustle and bustle below.

Circular Quay buzzed with activity, and people were waving as the ship pulled away from its berth, snapping the colourful streamers that bound it to shore. She had a great view from her vantage point: the Sydney Harbour Bridge on her left and the Opera House on her right as the ship sailed up the harbour. Both landmarks were imposing in the fading light.

The sound of low voices from somewhere on the deck above had her craning her head. If she had a great view from here, theirs must be amazing.

'Looks like loads of single women down there. Half are here for flings; the other half hope to find a husband. It's the same every cruise.'

'Your job is to pamper those women, not judge them.'

'Easy for you to say, buddy. If they see an unattached guy they're like piranhas circling their next meal.'

Despite her intentions to ignore the conversation, this harsh judgment captured Lana's attention, and realisation dawned as she looked up. Standing above her, silhouetted against the bridge, stood the stranger who'd saved her from falling earlier.

He wore a crisp white uniform that accentuated his tan—a larger than life Richard Gere in *An Officer and a Gentleman*—and she swallowed, disconcerted by how she'd compared him to two of her favourite movie stars in under an hour.

Deep furrows marred his brow as his gaze swept the crowd, and she shrank back, hoping she was hidden. She didn't want to be scrutinised by that disconcerting stare—not when she'd been eavesdropping, albeit unintentionally.

Mr Nautical's generalisations about women had her bristling enough to barge up there and give him a verbal spray, but if she had the guts to do that she'd be winging her way to Egypt right now, as the museum's spokesperson, not cowering under a deck hoping she wouldn't be spotted.

He was entitled to his opinion, and she to hers. And right now, as she darted a quick glance overhead, taking in those broad shoulders, deep blue eyes and the mop of unruly dark curls, her opinion screamed *Neanderthal.*

The band starting up drowned out the rest of his conversation, and she stood still for several minutes, waiting for the men above to move so she could make her escape without being seen. After a few extra minutes of shuffling her feet to kill time, she sidled along the deck, taking a few steps back towards an open door.

'Watch out!'

The owner of the low voice stood so close his warm breath caressed her ear, and she jumped and whirled around, her heart pounding as she stared into those familiar indigo eyes barely inches from her face.

'You startled me.' She glared, desperately trying to hide her embarrassment at being caught eavesdropping.

'Sorry. Maybe if you watched where you were going we'd stop bumping into each other like this? By the way—Zac McCoy.'

He stuck out his hand, seemingly unaware she'd heard every word of his damning conversation. She'd wanted to keep it that way, so couldn't be as rude as her first instinct prompted her to be.

'Lana Walker.'

She placed her hand in his, unprepared for the jolt that shot up her arm as his fingers closed over hers. She yanked back, flustered by the residual tingle buzzing from her fingertips to her shoulder.

His eyes widened as he stared down at her hand. Great. Now he thought she was bad-mannered as well as clumsy. Way to go with the first impressions. Not that she had any intention of impressing him after what she'd just heard— and as if she'd even contemplate impressing him if she hadn't, she thought derisively. Old clothes, minimal make-up and boring brown hair weren't exactly designed to impress any guy, let alone someone in Mr Tall, Dark and Nautical's league.

'I need to finish unpacking, so if you'll excuse me?'

As she pushed past him her bare arm brushed his. The strange buzzing was back with a vengeance, spreading upwards and outwards and confusing the heck out of her. She had no idea why her body was behaving like this.

Okay, so that was a lie. Jax the Jackass might have been her only boyfriend, the only guy she'd ever slept with, but once he'd dumped her and she'd fled to Sydney she'd had two less than memorable dates with co-workers. She still recognized that buzz.

Hormones. Her reaction to sailor boy had to be purely physical—no doubt intensified due to the fact she hadn't been this close to a guy in over three years.

'I'll leave you to it. Nice meeting you.'

She mumbled a non-committal answer and sent him a half-hearted wave, glancing over her shoulder as he walked away, her curious gaze lingering on parts it had no right scoping out.

She had a thing for guys in uniform. Always had.

Starting way back, when a young sailor had given her a flower after she'd dropped an ice cream cone and cried. A clumsy five-year-old who'd never forgotten her first crush. Her mum's warning at the time, to steer clear of men like that, hadn't meant much, considering she hadn't known what 'that' meant back then.

Now, seeing the white cotton outlining Zac McCoy's butt as he strode away, she knew exactly what *that* was, and it sent her scurrying for her cabin.

Banishing the encounter from her thoughts, she showered and dressed for dinner. Beth had crammed her case with designer dresses and shoes, but Lana would never have the self-confidence to wear half the sexy stuff her cousin did, so she settled for her one good dress: a plain black coat dress, cinched at the waist, set off with her cousin's sparkly jet Manolos.

Beth had pestered Lana to allow a complete makeover, but the thought of a radical haircut and new wardrobe was way too intimidating for a girl who equated the latest fashion with the occasional update of her tortoiseshell spectacle frames.

She'd settled for a sedate trim to her *blah*-brown hair and contacts. Beth had settled for giving her enough shoe cast-offs to make the *Sex and the City* girls sit up and take notice.

As for the rest of Beth's advice on how to boost her self-confidence? She'd take it one step at a time in these damn uncomfortable shoes.

She entered the Coral Dining Room and barely had time to notice the giant chandelier, the string quartet and the silver service place settings before the *maître d'* whisked her to a table where two seats remained vacant.

Sliding into one of them, she let the other occupants introduce themselves—a couple in their forties and two other women—hoping they wouldn't expect her to make small talk. She was lousy in social situations like this, preferring to sit and listen than participate in idle chit-chat.

She listened to their friendly banter while perusing the extensive menu. As the empty chair on her right was drawn back, her skin prickled disturbingly. A sensation she associated with the hives she'd been unfortunate enough to bear several times when a strawberry came within a whiff of her.

However, this prickle had nothing to do with fruit. This time something far more dangerous to her health—well, to her peace of mind—caused her skin to flush and tingle.

'Hi, everyone. I'm Zac McCoy, Public Relations Manager. I'm delighted you'll be joining me for meals at my table. On behalf of the ship's company, the Captain and the crew, we hope you enjoy your cruise.'

Fate liked to play jokes on her. Maybe she should take out a lottery ticket and be done with it.

Resisting the urge to surreptitiously scratch the flushed skin behind her ears, she tried to ignore her erratic pulse which had shifted into overdrive the minute he sat down. She toyed with the cutlery, pleated her napkin, and successfully avoided looking at him until the table introductions reached her.

'How are you, Lana?'

He flashed that killer smile, blue eyes glinting with amusement.

'Fine, thanks.'

That's it. Slay him with scintillating conversation. For a professional who gave presentations weekly—as painful as it was, speaking in front of her peers—she was doing a marvellous job appearing to be a brainless bimbo.

While the voluptuous blonde on his right distracted him,

she couldn't resist sneaking a peek. Smooth, suave and sexy. He was exactly the type of guy any sane woman would stay away from: a glib, good-looking charmer, with the body of Adonis and a face designed to turn heads. Way out of her league.

As dinner proceeded she remained silent, toying with her food, faking polite smiles. She'd never been a flirt, like Beth, and sitting next to a guy like Zac had her tongue-tied. Probably for the best, as she doubted he'd be interested in the latest marsupial display in the Australian Gallery, or in hearing her expound the virtues of digital cataloguing. Though her reticence was barely noticed as he maintained a steady flow of conversation, captivating everyone at the table.

During dessert—a light chocolate soufflé that melted in her mouth—he turned towards her.

'You're awfully quiet. Maybe we should get to know each other better?'

His bold stare scanned her face, focusing briefly on her mouth before returning to her eyes, and admiration tinged with something more—something that made her heart go pitter-patter—glittered in those blue depths.

'Maybe. Though I should warn you. I'm single, and probably hungrier than a piranha.'

His smile slipped as he dabbed at the corners of his mouth with a linen napkin, those vivid eyes never leaving hers for a second. She blinked to break the hypnotic contact.

'You overheard me earlier?'

'Yeah, and your opinion of women on cruises sucks.'

She silently applauded her bravado—fuelled by indignation—even while cringing at her outburst. Antagonising him wouldn't be conducive to remaining unnoticed, which was what she'd hoped for if she had to sit next to him every night for the next two weeks.

His eyes deepened to midnight, dark and challenging, as he leaned towards her.

'Care to change my mind?'

'And disillusion you because I'm not the man-hunter you think I am?' She eased back, needing some distance between them before she leaned into him and lapped up some of that delicious citrusy-sea-air scent he exuded. 'Where's the fun in that?'

'Oh, I think it could be fun,' he said.

His gaze dipped to her mouth again, lingered before sweeping back to her eyes. and she flicked her tongue out to moisten her lips, which tingled as if he'd physically touched her.

'And seeing as you think I'm a judgmental idiot, you would take a lot of convincing.' His voice dropped to a conspiratorial whisper. 'Which could equate to *a lot* of fun.'

'I didn't say you were an idiot.'

He chuckled—a rich, deep sound which washed over her in a warm wave. 'You didn't have to. You've got very expressive eyes.'

'Must be the contacts.'

Her dry response elicited more laughter.

'Look, I'd really like to clear the air between us. I honestly didn't mean anything by what you overheard. It was merely an observation from working on these tugs too long.'

She opened her mouth to respond and he held up a hand. 'Yes, it was a sweeping generalisation. And, yes, I'm suitably chastened and I apologise. But tell me, Lana Walker, which are you?'

He leaned closer. So close she couldn't breathe without imprinting his seductive scent on her receptors. 'Husband-hunter or fun fling girl?'

She reared back, knowing now was the time to clam up

as she usually did, before she scolded him like a tardy student. As she compressed her lips into an unimpressed line she noticed the teasing sparkle in his eyes, the cheeky smile playing about his mouth.

'You're trying to wind me up.'

'Is it working?'

'No.'

'So I could say anything and you'd be totally immune to me?'

Immune? She could have a hospital's worth of vaccinations against suave sailors and it still wouldn't give her guaranteed immunity—the type of immunity she needed more and more urgently the longer he stared at her with those twinkling eyes.

'That's right.'

'So I could say you intrigue me and you wouldn't react?'

'Nope.'

'What about if I tell you I think there's more to you than the obvious?'

She rolled her eyes. 'That's the same as intrigue, so you need to come up with a better line, sailor boy.'

'Sailor boy?'

A slow grin spread across his face as she mentally slapped a hand over her mouth.

Nicknames implied camaraderie. Nicknames implied fun. And there was no way she'd be foolish enough to *ever* contemplate having fun with him.

'Figure of speech.' She pleated her napkin, folding it over and over with origami-like precision, till he reached over and stilled her hand, setting her pulse rocketing as she tried not to flinch from his touch.

'What if I said I like you?'

Taking a great gulp of air to ease her constricted lungs,

she frowned. 'You're still trying to wind me up. And you're good. I'll give you that much.'

She extracted her hand on the pretext of picking up her wine glass, racking her brain for an easy way to end this conversation before she blurted out exactly how wound up she was by his teasing. The nape of her neck prickled. A colony of ants had taken up residence under her skin, and her blood flowed thick and sluggish, heating her from the inside out. Logically, she knew it was merely a physiological response—a simple chemical reaction to the first male to enter her personal space in a long time. But logic wouldn't untie her tongue or stop the rising blush from making her feel more gauche and awkward than ever in a social situation like this.

Smiling, he picked up his own wine glass and raised it in her direction.

'You do intrigue me. And I'm not trying to wind you up.' His smile widened. 'Well, not much. For some inexplicable reason I've taken an instant liking to you, despite your somewhat prickly exterior, and I've got two weeks to prove it to you.'

Prickly? The cheeky son of a—

He chuckled, and she knew he was winding her up again, trying to get a reaction.

She bit her tongue, mulling over what he'd said. He'd taken an instant liking to her, huh? As if. If she believed that she'd believe the ship would sail into the horizon and drop off the end of a flat earth.

Leaning forward, he murmured in her ear. 'Two very interesting weeks.'

She stiffened, unable to think when he was this close. What was the best response? Ignore him? Berate him? Wait the requisite ten minutes it would take to think up a scathing comeback and put him firmly back in his place?

'What? Nothing to say? Surprising, from a woman with such strong opinions about me.'

Sitting back, he fixed her with a smug smile—a smile that said he knew how flustered he made her, how she was struggling to come up with a suitable response.

She should have ignored him, pleaded a headache and left the table. That would have been her usual course of action—quietly slinking away, ruing her shyness. But his self-satisfied smile was too much, goading her into matching wits with him.

He assumed she couldn't come up with a quick answer? She'd show him.

So rather than pushing back her chair and making a run for it, she felt blood surge to her cheeks, and her head snapped up as she fixed him with a scathing glare.

'Go ahead, then, sailor boy. Prove it.'

CHAPTER TWO

LANA'S eyelids creaked open at the crack of dawn the next morning. A newly converted gym junkie, she usually bounced out of bed early and hit the nearest gym at six, when fitness fanatics liked to sweat through their first aerobics class of the day.

She'd never graced a gym, let alone tried an aerobics class, till eighteen months ago—all part of Operation Obliterate. Obliterate her memories of Jax, obliterate the embarrassment of how he'd used her; obliterate the fact that her first love had seen her as nothing more than a fling.

Now, not only was she hooked, she'd become a qualified instructor just for the fun of it. Madness? Probably. But for the hour she jumped around every morning she was just like the rest of the sweaty women around her, when no make-up and casual clothes weren't a big deal.

After a quick shower, she donned her favourite capri pants—in urgent need of replacing, considering the frayed cuffs—and a plain white T-shirt. She had a ton of them, as they went with everything. Then she slipped her feet into a pair of well-worn slingbacks.

Beth had shuddered when she'd seen her casual outfits, but, hey, she'd always been a comfort-over-style girl.

Besides, she didn't adhere to the old 'dress to impress' motto. She used her brain to get people to notice her. Discounting last night, when her intellect had gone AWOL.

Prove it, she'd dared Zac. All very brave in the heat of the moment, when she'd fired off the retort without thinking it through properly, but now, in the clear light of a perfect summer's day, her resolve wavered.

It was one thing setting out to build confidence by trying new things, but challenging a pro like Zac to flirt with her could only end in disaster.

He'd pushed her, taunted her till she'd snapped. He couldn't have known she'd react that way, for she still couldn't believe she'd done it herself. And while she now regretted her outburst, a small part of her was jumping up and down with joy at the unusual flash of bravado.

The old, sensible, conservative Lana would have ducked her head, pushed her ancient glasses up her nose and ignored him. She would have scuffed her well-worn sensible shoes under the table, tugged on the hem of her favourite shapeless sweatshirt and made a quick escape. She'd always taken the safe route, always done the right thing, always focussed on her career and nothing else.

She was the diligent employee, the dependable colleague, the model girlfriend, the reliable cousin. And where had it got her?

She'd been dumped, overlooked for a brilliant opportunity at work, and had come on this cruise for one reason and one reason only: to gain confidence socially and ensure she was never passed over at work again.

If she couldn't rely on her job, the one thing in this world she knew she was good at, what hope did she have?

Maybe standing up to brash sailors and proving she wasn't a push-over fell into the category of confidence-building?

With a shake of her head—as if that would dislodge the memory of making a fool of herself with that rash challenge—she headed for the lido deck, where continental breakfast was being served. She helped herself to a plate of mango, melon and pineapple, before finding a table next to the floor-to-ceiling glass overlooking the Pacific Ocean, stretching as far as she could see, its undulating swell infinitely soothing.

Her apartment in Coogee had an ocean view, though nothing as gorgeous as this. She'd deliberately chosen a sea view for its calming qualities and, boy, had she needed it when she'd first moved to Sydney from Melbourne, hell-bent on leaving her past behind.

'Enjoying the view this morning?'

She glanced up, her pulse-rate accelerating in an instant. Zac—in a navy polo shirt and matching shorts, his hair recently washed and slicked back, resident charming smile in place—rivalled the ocean in the stunning stakes.

She took a sip of water, trying to ease the dryness in her throat. 'Yes, it's spectacular.'

He wasn't looking at the view. Instead, that steady, captivating blue-eyed gaze remained riveted to her. 'Spectacular would describe it perfectly.'

She blushed and glanced down, toying with the fruit on her plate rather than face his intense scrutiny.

What made her think she could practise gaining confidence with this guy? He was a major player, and she'd barely graduated from Little League.

'You really should try some of that mango rather than playing with it. It's succulent this time of year.'

The way he said 'succulent' fascinated her; tripping from his lips, it almost sounded obscene.

'Shouldn't you be circulating amongst the passengers?'

She speared a piece of juicy mango and bit into it, trying to appear casual yet anxious to fob him off.

As if in slow motion he reached his index finger towards the corner of her mouth, where a rivulet of juice had started to run, and wiped it up.

Shaken to her core, she watched him lick the droplet of juice from his fingertip in a shockingly intimate gesture.

'Mmm—tasty.'

His smouldering gaze dropped to her lips before sweeping back to her eyes, triumphant blue clashing with shell-shocked hazel.

'You're right. I should get back to work. I can't have my time monopolized by one woman," he teased, before adding, 'Delectable as she may be.'

With a cocky smile, he gave her a half-salute and sauntered away.

The corner of her mouth was still quivering from his sensual touch. Great. If that was his first foray into *proving it* she was in trouble. Big trouble.

With a trembling hand she devoured the remainder of her breakfast, eager to escape. Whenever she looked up she caught a glimpse of him, moving among the tables, talking to various people. Their eyes met only once across the crowded room, and she looked away first, hating the blush staining her cheeks, hating her inadequacy at coping with light flirtation more.

It was hot in this room, way too hot. Pushing her plate away, she almost tripped in her haste to stand and dashed for the door, keeping her head down, unwilling to tempt fate further. After virtually falling into his arms, landing next to him at dinner, and then running into him first thing this morning, it looked as if fate was having a mighty big chuckle at her expense.

* * *

Zac watched Lana bolt, hiding a triumphant grin as he flipped the pages on his clipboard. He had her thoroughly rattled, if that stunned, wide-eyed gaze when he'd touched her lips was any indication.

Maybe he'd pushed the boundaries a tad there, but he hadn't been able to help it; he wanted to see if anything disturbed that cool-bordering-on-haughty mantle she wore like a fine fur.

He'd disconcerted her last night to the point where she'd thrown out that challenge. He was in little doubt she would never have been that brazen, that sassy, if she'd been thinking straight. After all, a woman who turned up to her first dinner on a luxurious cruise liner wearing a drab black dress with oversized buttons, a God-awful belt, and barely a slick of make-up, and who rarely spoke, wasn't exactly brimming with confidence.

Yet he'd wanted to push her buttons anyway.

Must be the pressure. He had a job to do, a saboteur to uncover, and some bad publicity to bring to a screaming halt. His uncle was relying on him, and he owed Jimmy big-time. He'd let him down once. Never again.

He needed to concentrate on business—needed to convince everyone he was just the new PR guy. The success of his plan depended on it. Even if he was actually the CEO of the whole damn company, and usually had bigger fish to fry.

And concentrating on business meant not giving Lana a hard time—challenge or not. Though there had been something about the spark in her eyes when she'd fired back at him last night, something about her wary yet indignant expression that had him wanting to delve beneath her prim surface to discover the hidden depths.

Maybe if he unnerved her enough, unsettled her enough, he'd get to see the real her?

An interesting proposition, but for now work came first. Work was reliable, dependable, and never let him down. It wasn't clouded by emotions and it didn't change when he least expected it. Work was the one constant in his life. The only constant.

Exactly the way he liked it.

Lana studied *Neptune's News,* the ship's daily planner, as she lounged around the lido pool, staggered by the array of activities on board: lectures on ports they were due to visit, wine-tasting, art auctions, dance lessons—the list went on for ever. She studiously avoided any activities with Zac's name pencilled next to them, and finally decided on ballroom dancing—something she'd always wanted to try but never had the guts to. Hopefully mastering a waltz or two might give her a quickstep in the right direction to boosting her self-confidence.

Finding her way to the ballroom proved easier said than done. Maps were clearly visible around the ship, but understanding the difference between port and starboard was the first hurdle to overcome in figuring out directions, and only after several botched attempts did she finally find the room. So much for her sure-fire navigational skills; apparently they only applied to the maze of one-way streets around Sydney and to convoluted museum corridors.

Several women stood to one side of the ballroom, while a few men loitered on the outskirts of the dance floor. She learned from Mavis, the woman standing next to her, that the men were hosts, hired by the ship's company for single women who needed a dance partner.

'This is my seventh cruise, dear. Why do you think I

keep coming back? Though I'm seventy, these dance hosts make me feel twenty-one again, whisking me all over the dance floor. Not to mention their youthful good-looks.'

Lana smothered a smile as the youngest host appeared to be a greying fifty-five. She observed that the men were skilled at mingling with the women, and soon everyone had paired off. Predictably, she had no partner. Story of her life, really.

'Don't worry, love, you'll be the lucky one paired with the instructor.'

Mavis, veteran cruiser, obviously knew how these things worked.

'I hope he's good.'

Because she was a dervish out there on the dance floor? Yeah, right. She moved her feet to an imaginary samba rhythm and almost took a tumble.

'I'm better than good. Let's just hope you can keep up.'

Her nerve-endings snapped to attention as the deep voice rippled over her, and she didn't have to turn around to know who it belonged to. Fickle fate dealing her a bum hand yet again.

'Okay, class, let's get to work. As you can see, I'm not Rafe, our illustrious dance instructor. He was called away to a last-minute rehearsal for tonight's extravaganza, so you're stuck with me instead. For those who don't know me, I'm Zac McCoy, the PR manager. Though I'm not a professional entertainer, I can safely say I don't have two left feet, and I've managed to learn a thing or two during my years working with the entertainment staff. So, how about a waltz to start with?'

'Anything you want, handsome. Oh, if only I was thirty years younger.' Mavis fanned her face, a twinkle in her eyes.

'If only I'd decided on taking the chess class,' Lana muttered, wondering if she could feign a sprained ankle.

'Did you say something?'

She had two choices. Duck and run, as she usually would in an uncomfortable situation like this, or ignore the blush burning her cheeks, discount the fact she'd never done this before, and suck it up and see if she could get through this awkward encounter without making a fool of herself.

She shook her head, managing a tight smile resembling a grimace. 'No.'

'Right, then. Shall we dance?'

Zac grinned and held out his hand, leaving her no option but to take it. She tried to relax, she really did, but as he pulled her closer, his body grazing hers, she inadvertently stiffened.

His knowing smile didn't help. 'See—a perfect fit.'

'I thought we were doing a waltz. The way you're holding me seems more like the Lambada.'

'Fancy a bit of dirty dancing, do you?'

'Don't flatter yourself. You certainly don't hold a candle to Patrick Swayze.'

A glint of hidden excitement lit his extraordinary eyes.

'And here I was thinking you were falling under my spell. You disappoint me.'

She averted her gaze, focussing on anything other than those all-seeing eyes, wishing her heart would stop racing. 'Don't you ever stop flirting?'

His grin widened. 'I'm sure Fred did his fair share of flirting while he whisked Ginger around. I'm just taking my role seriously.'

'Your role as the resident Casanova, you mean?'

The naughty glint in his eyes alerted her to the fact she hadn't insulted him. Moreover, he was enjoying their sparring way too much.

'We're both adults here. There's nothing wrong with a bit of harmless flirtation. Besides, you dared me—remember?'

More fool her.

'Look, this is silly. You were taunting me last night. I bit back. Let's just forget it, okay?

The naughty glint didn't let up. If anything it intensified as his lips kicked up into an all too sexy grin.

'Unfortunately for you I have a very good memory, so I can't forget it. But I'm willing to concentrate on our dance steps for now.' And with that he spun her outwards, at arm's length.

'If that's your way of changing the subject, I'm not buying it.'

He reeled her in with a slight tug on her hand. 'Who said anything about needing to change the subject? I enjoy flirting. You're the one with the problem.'

If he only knew.

She didn't know how to flirt—had absolutely no experience at it. Jax had targeted her, played her, said all the right things—done all the right things to get her to fall for him. Flirting hadn't entered into it. As for her other two dates, they'd been stilted, awkward, rushed dinners, with limited small talk and frequent glances at watches on both sides.

It wasn't so much having a problem with flirting, she just didn't have a clue how to do it.

She stumbled, winced, trod on his toes, and wished the parquet floor would open up and swallow her.

'Easy, Ginger. Just follow my lead.'

If he'd smiled or smirked or had the faintest amused twinkle in his eyes she would have slammed her heel on his foot—well, she would have thought about it—and made a run for it.

Instead, he tightened his hold on her hand, gently increased the pressure with the other in the small of her back, and counted softly under his breath as he led her around the dance floor.

The counting was for her benefit, but it didn't help. Clumsy, stiff and awkward didn't begin to describe how she felt in his arms—like a mannequin given an airing before being dumped in a shopfront in only her knickers.

Thinking of knickers while in his arms had her trampling his toes again, and she bit her lip, silently cursing her ineptness.

'Sorry.'

Her gaze fixed on his chest, heat scorching her cheeks.

He stopped twirling her about, placed a finger under her chin and tilted it up so she had no option but to look at him.

'Don't apologise. This class is about learning, and you're doing great for a beginner.'

His understanding smile sent a tremor through her. Why couldn't he be condescending and obnoxious so she could dislike him, rather than considerate and kind?

She mumbled a noncommittal answer, wishing he'd stop staring at her like a pet project. Though it could be worse; he could be looking down on her as a charity case with pity in his eyes.

'Just feel the music. Let the beat take you.'

Easy for Fred Astaire Junior to say.

Her dubious expression had him chuckling as he pulled her closer again. 'Come on. You'll enjoy it.'

To her surprise, he was right. As soon as she stopped focussing on her feet not stomping on his, and ignored the fact he was holding her close, she started to relax.

The music filtered over her, soft and ethereal, a classical hit from a bygone era, and she found herself humming softly, swept away in the magic of the moment.

She closed her eyes, remembered a dancing show she'd

once seen on TV, and imagined herself in a red chiffon dress with a fitted bodice held up by will-power alone, with handkerchief layers cascading from her waist to her ankles. She imagined snazzy red shoes to match, sequinned, with impossibly high heels, that floated across the dance floor of their own volition.

With immaculate hair and make-up, and the smile of a ballroom dancing champion, she lived the fantasy, let the music infuse her body, her senses, and allowed Zac to whisk her around and around, her feet finally falling into step with his as an exhilaration she'd never known rushed through her.

She'd never felt so light, so graceful, so unselfconscious. If this was what ballroom dancing could do for her, she'd sign up for a year's worth of classes as soon as she got back.

But there was more to it than perfecting a waltz and she knew it.

Zac had given her this gift—had given her the confidence to let go of her reservations and enjoy the moment. He'd empowered her to believe that for a precious few minutes she could be agile and lithe and elegant, rather than a shy, clumsy klutz.

When the music died her eyelids fluttered open, but rather than feeling let down by reality, the gleam of appreciation in his deep blue eyes had her craving to do it all over again.

'You're good.'

His admiration made her want to perform a few extra twirls for good measure.

She flushed with pleasure. 'Thanks. So are you.'

'You up for a cha-cha?'

Ignoring the usual flicker of nerves at the thought of trying something new, she nodded. 'Sure. Let's give it a try.'

Not only did she try a cha-cha, Zac showed her the finer

points of a foxtrot too. While the class danced around them, she matched him step for step, exhilarated by his fancy manoeuvres, thrilled by her increasing confidence to try more complicated steps.

At the end of the hour she collapsed into a nearby chair, her face flushed, her feet aching and her imagination still tripping the light fantastic.

He crouched next to her as she puffed at the damp hair strands falling over her face, knowing she must look a hot, rumpled mess. Yet a small part of her was still feeling like that dance champion she'd imagined.

'You're just full of surprises, aren't you, Ginger?'

'Why? Because I only managed to break all the toes on your right foot and not your left?'

He laughed. 'You'll be pleased to know my toes are just fine. Better than fine, considering I had to do some fancy footwork out there to keep up with you once you got going.'

There was a reason he was in PR. He probably laid it on this thick for countless other gullible females every cruise.

'Yeah, well, I told you I was good at the start.' His eyebrows shot up as he clearly relived every clumsy stumble she'd made initially and she smiled. 'And you're not such a bad teacher, once you concentrate on the task at hand and put a zip on the banter.'

'Thanks. I think.' He stood, stretched, and she quickly averted her gaze from the window of tanned, flat stomach poking between his polo shirt and shorts. 'See you tonight at dinner?'

His smile was pure invitation. If he'd asked her a few hours ago she would have sent him a short, sharp RSVP in the negative, but after the enlivening hour she'd just spent, thanks to him, she found herself nodding.

'Uh-huh.'

'Right-o. See you then.'

She fanned her cheeks as he walked away, wondering if it was the exercise, the exhilaration of feeling graceful for the first time in her life, or being wrapped in his muscular arms that had made her hot and bothered?

In reality she should be happy—ecstatic, even. She'd tried something new today and had given her flagging confidence a much-needed lift. Her sense of achievement was immense, and she owed it to one guy.

And now she'd experienced the rush of feeling graceful for the first time in her life she wondered how much further he could boost her confidence—if she didn't try so hard to fend him off.

CHAPTER THREE

WHILE Zac had impressed her with his sensitivity during dance class yesterday, he had ruined it by slipping into full flirting mode over dinner last night. Her fledgling confidence hadn't lasted and she'd clammed up, grunted monosyllabic answers, and done her best to ignore the persistent attentions of a suave sailor boy with smooth moves and slick words.

She hated the fact it was a game to him, a response to the challenge she'd thrown down in a fit of pique. Her inherent shyness was a bane she lived with every day, it affected her professionally, socially and romantically, yet he seemed to view it as something she could shrug off if he teased her enough.

He was really starting to get to her, but thankfully the ship had docked at Noumea today, and she wouldn't waste another minute thinking about him. Instead, she explored the French-inspired capital of New Caledonia, with its tree-lined boulevards flanked by trendy boutiques and cafés, enjoying every minute.

She savoured the aroma of freshly brewed coffee wafting on the light tropical breeze, she scoffed melt-in-the-mouth flaky croissants, and she scoured the shops—something she never did back home. When she shopped it was for necessity rather than a burning need for retail therapy—no matter how many times Beth dragged her from one boutique to another trying to make her see otherwise.

Yet here, with the balmy breeze ruffling her ponytail and the tempting shopfronts laid out like bright, sparkling jewels in the sun, she couldn't help but browse.

Entering a small boutique, she meandered through aisles crammed with enough hangers and clothes to outfit the entire cast of *South Pacific*. Her hands drifted over soft silky sarongs, short strappy summer dresses, before lingering over the swimwear. The only bathers she'd brought on this trip were an old black one-piece cut high in the front—the ones she used if she swam at home as part of a workout.

So why was she picking up a cerise bikini, its hot pink colour the exact shade her cheeks would be if she ever had the guts to wear something so revealing?

She put it down and trailed her hand over some straw hats, before her gaze settled on the bikini again, drawn to it, mesmerised by its newness, its brightness and its blinding contrast to everything else in her wardrobe.

Glancing down at her worn black flip-flops, khaki Bermuda shorts and well-washed grey T-shirt, she hovered over the bikini, sorely tempted. Just looking at it gave her the same buzz she'd had when floating around the dance floor in Zac's arms—the feeling she could be more assertive if she set her mind to it.

Spurred on by an eagerness to recreate that feeling, she snatched it up and headed for the counter before she changed her mind.

After thrusting the bikini at the young Melanesian guy behind the counter, she ducked her head on the pretext of searching for her purse in her straw carryall, hating how her cheeks burned when making what was a simple, every-day purchase for most women.

She rummaged around, waiting for him to ring it up, and was unprepared for the small puff of perfume in the vicinity of her right ear.

'This fragrance will be perfect for *mademoiselle*.'

She shook her head, ready to tell him she wasn't interested, when an intoxicating blend of light floral tones mingling with subtle vanilla drifted over her. She inhaled, savouring the heady scent, feeling surprisingly feminine after one small squirt.

She never wore perfume, had never owned a bottle in her life, but when the young guy stared at her with soulful chocolate-brown eyes and insisted again that it was perfect for her, in a divine French accent, she found herself handing over her credit card and being handed back a duty-free bag with two purchases she'd never dreamed of making, let alone using.

But for those few minutes when she'd watched him wrap the bikini and the perfume she'd stood a little taller, felt a little braver—as if she could be the type of woman who *wasn't* passed over for an amazing trip to Egypt as the museum's spokesperson just because she wasn't articulate or outgoing enough.

However, her flash of spirit didn't last as she strolled back to the ship. The perfume box banged against her leg, a constant reminder of its presence, and she couldn't help but feel a fool.

Since when did she wear perfume? Let alone go for something so…so…out there? Seductive, feminine items were for girls not short on confidence—girls who'd have the guts to live up to the perfume's promise; girls who'd have the spirit to match wits with sailor boys. Girls absolutely nothing like her.

Impulse buying a stupid perfume with a naughty name wouldn't give her the confidence boost she needed. Nothing would. And she'd be better off remembering that rather than entertaining foolish dreams of showing everyone, Zac included, that she wasn't the shy nerd they'd labelled her.

When she got back to her cabin, she flung the duty-free bag into the wardrobe and slammed the door shut.

Ruing the waste of money—as if she'd *ever* have the chutzpah to wear that bikini—she wriggled into her trusty one-piece and headed for the Dolphin Deck pool. She dumped her towel and sarong on a deckchair before plunging into the water, eager to wash away memories of her recent foolishness.

Closing her eyes, she flipped over, floating blissfully until a dark shadow passed over her. When it didn't move, she opened her eyes.

And promptly sank.

Torn between the natural urge to fight her way to the surface for air or stay submerged, safely away from charming sailor boys, she eventually floundered her way to the surface, spluttering and coughing and ruining her Esther Williams impersonation.

'Need a hand?'

She glared at his outstretched hand and shook her head, deriving some satisfaction as water droplets sprayed his immaculate uniform.

'No, thanks.'

His lips curved into a deliciously tempting smile. 'You sure? Not tempted to try and pull me in?'

The thought hadn't crossed her mind, but now he mentioned it maybe a good dunking would cool him off.

'Not really. And I'm quite capable of hoisting myself out of the pool—if you'd move out of my way?'

'I like a strong woman.'

She rolled her eyes. 'You like women, period.'

'What's wrong with that? I'm a healthy red-blooded male.'

Her gaze drifted across his broad shoulders of its own volition, and lower, before snapping back to meet his all too sure of himself stare.

'I'll take your word for it.'

She pushed away from the side of the pool, treading water, floundering out of her depth physically and literally. Ever since she'd been silly enough to dare him that first night he'd been teasing her, pushing her for a reaction.

'As much as I'm enjoying your mermaid impersonation, why don't you come a little closer so we can have a proper chat?'

'About…?'

'Tonight. You and me.'

How did he do that? Infuse every word with mystery and mayhem and untold promise? As if his sexy smile and come-get-me eyes weren't enough.

For the second time in as many minutes she went under, cursing her inability to be anything other than clumsy and inept in his presence. He unnerved her to the point of bumbling, and it was high time she got over this funk he had her in with his constant teasing. Either that or jump ship.

She breaststroked underwater to the side, and hauled herself up the pool ladder. 'Don't say a word. Just hand me that towel, please.'

He was smart as well as good-looking, for he didn't speak as he passed her the towel. Then again, he didn't need to. His smug smile said it all.

He had her squirming, wanting to match wits with him, wishing she could, but scared of the consequences. Her heart was slamming against her ribcage at the thought of what they might entail.

For some strange reason he'd fixated his charms on her this cruise. Her—the last woman who'd reciprocate, the last woman to put up with his nonsense, the last woman to dally with if that was his intention.

She wasn't a dallying type of girl, yet with him staring at her with a twinkle in those deep blue eyes it was hard not to wish she was.

'Aren't you at all interested to hear what I have in mind for you and me tonight?'

Oh, she was interested all right—interested to the point she'd almost drowned when he'd strung the words *you, me and tonight* into the same sentence.

Tying her sarong around her waist, having quickly patted herself dry, she aimed for casual. 'I'm sure you'll tell me.'

He chuckled. 'Nice to see you this wound up. It must mean I'm getting somewhere in my quest to prove how much I like you.'

'I'm not wound up.'

She finished tying the knot at her waist with an extra hard yank, almost cutting off her circulation in the process.

'No?'

He sent a pointed stare at the twisted mess she'd made of her sarong, and she stopped fiddling with it, crossing her arms instead.

Bad move, considering the wicked gleam in his eyes as he dragged them away from her cleavage.

'I just wanted to make sure you're coming to the Island Banquet. You won't want to miss it.'

'That good, huh?'

'Better.'

His lowered tone indicated he wasn't just talking about

the banquet. See, this was where she struggled. She had no idea if he was being clever or flirty or deliberately naughty—no idea how to respond without sounding repressed and uptight or foolishly naïve.

'Well, then, I look forward to seeing your prowess at organising events.'

'I'm sure you won't be disappointed with my *prowess*.'

He took a step towards her and ran his hand lightly down her arm. She shivered, tiny goosebumps crawling across her skin as she belatedly realised she'd given him the upper hand yet again.

'That's a promise.'

Oh, he was good—too good. She should just hoist her white flag up the main pole now in surrender.

He'd won. He'd bombarded her with enough smooth moves and clever words to prove he liked her. Though it was just a game to him, and she knew it. Then why the urge to ignore her head, the logical part of her that she always listened to, the part telling her to jump ship now before she was sucked into believing any of this was real?

'See you tonight.' His husky tone washed over her like a warm wave, soft, soothing, seductive, and he grazed her arm in a fleeting touch before walking away, leaving her helpless and yearning and cursing her inexperience with men more than ever.

Lana needed a shot of confidence, and in the absence of a ballroom dancing class she settled for a squirt of that frivolous perfume.

Considering her hand still shook as she pulled a brush through her hair it hadn't worked and she contemplated staying in and ordering Room Service rather than face another inevitable encounter with Zac.

Her nerves were shredded. She couldn't pretend to be someone she wasn't, and standing up to his incessant beguiling barrage could wear her down eventually. She couldn't handle that.

As she strolled towards the huge marquee about a mile from the ship, where the banquet was being held, the warm trade winds ruffled the hair at the nape of her neck. She knew wearing a new perfume and hoping it would give her poise while under duress was wishful thinking.

Fear settled in the pit of her stomach. Pep-talks to herself, telling her to stay cool and not let him rattle her, were fine in the confines of her cabin, but how would she stand up under pressure from his persistent charm?

Smoothing her old formal dress with nervous hands, she entered the marquee, where suspended fairy lights created a magical effect as they reflected in the water. Tables lined the outskirts, heavily laden with local seafood delicacies, salads and decadent desserts, and she tried not to drool. Easy, considering a certain sailor boy was nowhere in sight.

Mavis, resplendent in a floral dress with an orange hibiscus tucked behind her right ear, sidled up to her, beaming as usual. 'Aloha, dear.'

Lana didn't have the heart to tell her the Hawaiian greeting wasn't used here. 'You're looking very tropical.'

'Yes, well, we've got to get into the island spirit, haven't we? By the way, where's your beau? I haven't seen him.'

'My beau?'

Mavis tut-tutted. 'Don't play coy with me, my girl. I saw the way that sailor looked at you yesterday in dance class. I may be old, but I'm far from senile, and if my eyes didn't deceive me I think you liked the attention.'

'No way—'

'Why don't you live a little? Have some fun, dear.

You're only young once. Now, in order to do that you need to keep mingling and stop wasting your time talking to an old chook like me.' She patted Lana's cheek. 'Say hello to that gorgeous boy for me,' she said and waddled away, chuckling under her breath

Have some fun. You're only young once.

She wanted to, she really did, but ignoring the habits of a lifetime was tough. Even if she knew how to flirt, would Zac be satisfied with that? She doubted it. If she responded he'd take it as a signal that she was interested in more, would probably expect more, and she couldn't give it to him.

She was anti-casual-sex for a reason, a damn good one, and casting off her inhibitions along with her reservations would be near impossible.

Unless she had great motivation?

Maybe she did—all wrapped up in six-foot-plus of sexy sailor. Was Zac incentive enough for her to drop her guard and see where it led?

The thought had her bolting from the marquee for the safety of the deserted beach, where she could quash daft thoughts like that before they blossomed and encouraged her to indulge in all kinds of crazy, uncharacteristic actions.

Zac made small talk with a couple from Alabama while his gaze was riveted on Lana as she left the marquee.

He was an expert at multi-tasking—his job, his *real* job, demanded it—so he had no trouble nodding and laughing and responding even while hiding a grimace at yet another hideous dress, this one in a drab brown, and at the way it hid her curves.

And she had them—man, did she have them. He'd seen them on full display this afternoon, despite that neck-to-knee ensemble. Okay, it hadn't been that bad, but those boring bathers were gruesome just the same, and she no doubt thought they hid the curves that could give a guy ideas of how far he'd like to push this challenge, despite his every intention not to.

She'd come to the banquet. He'd had his doubts after the way he'd taunted her at the pool earlier. She was still nervous around him—something he couldn't figure out, considering she'd come alive in his arms in that dance class after she'd loosened up, and the way she'd started smiling at some of his jokes over dinner.

Socialising didn't come naturally to her. He saw it in the fiddling fingers, the tense shoulders, the lowered gaze whenever his flirting got too heated. He should feel sorry for her, should leave her alone.

An image of her in that wet, clinging, black one-piece sprang to mind again, instantly obliterating his good intentions to keep his distance. The bathing suit hadn't been remotely sexy, but the woman in it—now, that was another story.

All afternoon he'd mentally rehearsed the reasons he shouldn't push this: the 'employees don't fraternise with passengers' policy he'd devised himself; the importance of focussing on the quest to catch their saboteur; the debt he owed Uncle Jimmy. All perfectly legitimate reasons to keep his distance and stop toying with her—not to mention the fact she hadn't returned his interest in the slightest.

But he couldn't get her out of his head. He'd never met anyone like her: fragile, shy, clumsy and yet infinitely endearing. Quite simply, she captivated him.

It couldn't be purely physical, not with the dreadful clothes she wore—old-fashioned clothes that hid her body rather than enhancing it. And she rarely wore make-up, she tied her hair in a ponytail most of the time, and she wore no jewellery.

But that was what intrigued him the most: her apparent lack of artifice, which allowed the natural intelligent sparkle of her expressive eyes to shine through, and her genuine smile on the rare occasion one of his funny barbs hit its mark with her.

Her acerbic wit attracted him—the guarantee she wouldn't put up with any of his crap. He liked that enough to know more, a lot more, and now, with curiosity egging him on, he bade goodbye to the couple and followed her.

The soft sand silenced his footsteps, and he pulled up as she stopped at the ocean's edge, rubbing her arms before wrapping them around her middle. It was a vulnerable gesture that had him wondering who or what had put the wary expression in her eyes that he'd glimpsed on more than one occasion.

For someone her age—he'd pegged her as mid to late twenties—she was too serious, too withdrawn, and each time he'd seen caution creep into her striking hazel eyes he'd wanted to slay whatever demon had put it there.

Crazy, considering his demon-slaying days for any woman were long gone. Magda had seen to that.

Her posture screamed *hands-off* so what was he doing here, disturbing her solitude? Up for another bout of flirting? Another bout of teasing her when he knew it couldn't lead anywhere? She'd made that pretty clear.

He needed to leave her the hell alone. But before he could take a step the breeze picked up, and a waft of fragrance assailed his nostrils. He inhaled, savouring the tantalising scent of frangipani with a hint of vanilla. Pure ambrosia, piquant and addictive. He shook his head to clear it.

He must have made a noise, for she turned, pale moonlight casting alluring shadows over a face otherwise bathed in luminosity, her eyes wide and incandescent.

He'd never seen anything so stunning. The impact of her simple beauty hit him like a blow to the solar plexus, and for an oxygen-starved moment all he could do was stare.

'Sneaking up on me again?'

The slight curve of her lips belied the hint of annoyance in her voice.

'You look like you could do with some company.'

'Maybe.'

'Really?'

'Don't sound so surprised. You're not too bad for a persistent pain in the butt.'

He laughed, surprised she'd instigated a bit of light-hearted wordplay for the first time.

'Be careful. That almost sounded like a compliment, and it might go straight to my head.'

'Which part? The persistent pain part or the part where I actually admitted you're not too bad?'

'Take a guess.'

She smiled, and the effect was breathtaking. 'I'm sure you're well aware of your attributes, so anything I say isn't going to surprise you too much.'

'My attributes, huh?' He flexed his biceps, straightened his shoulders. 'Nice to know you noticed.'

She rolled her eyes. 'See? I knew it'd go to your head.'

He chuckled and closed the short distance between them, ducking his head towards her neck. 'What's that perfume, by the way? It's entrapment for any male who gets within five feet of you. Look at me; I'm putty in your hands at the moment.'

'It's called Seduction. Stupid name, but it smells okay. I bought it today in a fit of madness.'

She'd stiffened imperceptibly at his nearness, meaning he should probably leave her alone.

But he couldn't.

Not when the word Seduction tripped from her lips like a saucy invitation. Not when the word conjured up all sorts of wicked images in his over-heated imagination. Not when she smelt and looked divine under a star-studded sky just made for romance and frivolity and getting swept away in the moment.

'Seduction, huh?'

Her small nod brought her ear within nibbling range, and he gritted his teeth, straightening, removing delectable necks and ears out of temptation's way—only to catch the flicker of awareness warring with indecision in her un-wavering stare.

'I couldn't resist it.'

'Like I can't resist this.'

He lowered his lips towards her as her eyelids fluttered shut, the faint pink staining her cheeks adding a natural glow.

He half expected her to push him away, and her tenta-tive acceptance of his kiss surprised him, pleased him, considering her usual reticence for anything beyond the mildest flirtation.

He'd wanted to do this for days, yet the anticipation of her lips touching his didn't compare to the reality.

As he rested his hands on her waist, spanning it, she combusted.

There was no other description for her reaction as she wrapped her arms around him, tugging him closer, her hands frantic as they bunched his shirt, stroked his back, raking it while pushing against him, eager and spontane-ous and incredibly responsive.

He deepened the kiss, demanding a compliance she was

more than willing to give, and her total abandonment fired his libido better than any aphrodisiac as she parted her lips, allowing his tongue to slide into her mouth, where it wound around hers in an erotic, sensual dance he didn't want to end.

Blistering heat scorched straight to his groin and he groaned, threading his hands through her silky soft hair, loose and cascading over her shoulders for once, angling her head for better access to the warm delights of her mouth, wanting more, wanting it all.

He knew he shouldn't be doing this. It defied logic, defied all reason. But her tongue touching his blasted every last shred of common sense out of his mind.

As her breasts pressed against his chest and her hands skimmed the waistband of his trousers sanity fled, and he tore his mouth away, blazing a trail of hot, moist kisses down her throat.

Her head fell back, giving him full access to her neck and her deliciously delicate skin, so soft, so enticing, so tempting.

He couldn't get enough, cupping her butt, pulling her against his arousal, wishing their damn clothes would disappear along with her inhibitions.

Lana gasped, her eyes flying open as the enormity of what they were doing hit her like a ten-ton anchor.

What the hell was she thinking?

Trying to hold her own with his flirting was one thing—but this? This mind-blowing madness where she'd responded to him like a nympho?

The heat that had pooled in her belly crept upwards, causing her neck to itch uncontrollably and her cheeks to light a beacon for the ship.

How could she have been so…so…stupid? So wanton? So reckless?

She shoved her hair out of the way, dragged air into her lungs and stepped away, desperate for physical distance where a moment ago she couldn't get close enough.

His mouth kicked up into a rueful smile. 'Guess that perfume almost lived up to its name.'

Soft moonlight reflected in his eyes, and while she couldn't fathom their expression, she knew hers was horrified.

'In your dreams, lover-boy.'

She blinked, wondering where that rapid retort had come from. The quick comeback had shocked her almost as much as her eager response to his kiss.

To her amazement he chuckled—a deep, rich sound that had no right warming her. 'I guess here's where I should say it was my fault and that the kiss was way out of line.'

Her head snapped up, her stare accusing.

'You're right on both counts—but you're not going to apologise, are you? You've been charming the pants off me ever since I issued that stupid dare, so the way your warped mind works you probably think of it as all part of the game.'

'Charming the pants off you, huh?'

He dropped his gaze to her dress, and she blushed before jabbing a finger at him.

'You're incorrigible, you know that?'

'So I've been told.'

He grabbed her finger, lowered it, taking the opportunity to hold her hand, strumming the back of it with his thumb, soothing her anger just when she was getting worked up. Anger was good. Anger was distracting. Much better than focussing on the other emotions whirling through her: wonder and awe and a soul-deep yearning to feel half as good now as she had for those brief seconds in his arms.

'What do you want to hear? That I've wanted to kiss you for days? Damn straight. Do I want a repeat? Hell, yeah.'

A few of Jax's parting shots echoed through her head: *frigid, frosty, aloof, cold.* How could she be any of those things when a kiss from Zac set her alight and he wanted a repeat performance?

But it couldn't happen again. Not when Jax's other comments still resonated: how their relationship had been a bit of fun, nothing serious, a fling. She'd given him her heart; he'd given her a case of dating stage-fright for the next three years. There was no way she'd ever get involved with a guy again without having the relationship parameters spelled out at the start.

As if a transient sailor boy who lived his life at sea would be interested in anything more than a fling.

She yanked her hand out of his, folded her arms. 'A repeat is not an option.' She frowned for good measure, her old prickly exterior firmly back in place. 'It was a mistake. Just forget it.'

He shook his head, the hint of a smile curving those incredible lips she'd never forget. 'Impossible.'

Great. Was he referring to not repeating the kiss or forgetting it? No way was she asking for clarification.

With her head a riotous confusion of thoughts and her heart a frightening jumble of emotions, she knew she had to escape. Fast.

Her usual shyness wasn't justification for this desperate need to run. This had more to do with the growing horror that she'd totally embarrassed herself by kissing him like a sex-starved Playboy Bunny, and the deep, unshakeable fear she'd like to do it again.

'I have to go.'

She didn't wait for a response. Kicking off her shoes,

scooping them up with trembling hands, she made a mad dash across the sand, wishing she could flee the memories of her insane response to his kiss as easily.

CHAPTER FOUR

LANA tossed and turned all night, haunted by a tall, dark sailor with piercing blue eyes who commanded her dreams in explicit erotic detail.

Sleep-deprived and grumpy, she rolled out of bed at six, needing an aerobics class more than ever to work off some of her pent-up frustration. It worked back home, when she had to unwind after dealing with missing freight or junior staff with non-existent people skills, so why not here?

Zac had kissed her.

And she'd let him.

Worse, she'd responded, lost control for an insane moment in time, dropping her guard for a pair of persuasive blue eyes and a dashing smile.

She never dropped her guard—not since discovering Jax's deception, not since he'd dumped her and trampled her hopes for a future in the process.

It was why she didn't go in for fancy clothes or make-up, or snazzy highlights in her hair. She was comfortable in her own skin, secure in using her bland appearance as a protective mechanism to ward off guys after more than she could give.

But Zac didn't seem to care. It was as if he saw past her

dreary dresses and sloppy T-shirts, as if he saw the real her: a woman with needs, a woman who wanted to break free of her conservative mould but was too damn scared to try.

How ironic. He'd caught her off-guard and she'd given in to temptation, her burgeoning confidence courtesy of the dance class and the perfume purchase retreating faster than the First Fleet under siege.

Now she had to deal with the aftermath of that scorching kiss and her cringe-worthy sex-starved reaction. Ensure she forgot it and make damn sure it never happened again.

Once dressed, she headed for the gym. Exercising was familiar, exercising was cathartic, and exercising would surely burn off the energy buzzing through her body since she'd lip-locked Zac McCoy.

She needed to stop dwelling, stop replaying it in her head. It had happened; she couldn't take it back. Now she needed to move on, protective armour firmly in place again.

Determined to stop brooding, she strode into the small gym, crammed with about twenty ladies of varying shape, age and attire warming up on exercise bikes and treadmills.

Some of her tension dissipated in an instant at the comforting familiarity, and she found a space, dropped her towel and started stretching. She was midway through a hamstring stretch, her leg resting on a bar with her head almost touching her knee, when the instructor entered.

She froze, her hamstring giving a nasty twang as her leg slipped from the bar when Zac strode past, barely breaking stride.

Oh, no. Seeing him now was too soon, too awkward, too much.

He faced the room and twenty women sighed in unison. She didn't—she was supposed to be forgetting last night—but she couldn't blame them. Not with him standing there looking decidedly sigh-worthy in navy shorts, white polo shirt, his ever-present charming smile in place.

'Good morning, ladies. I can see you're all keen to start working out if you're up this early. Unfortunately Shelley had an accident ashore last night, and has a severely sprained ankle. So I'm sorry, but these classes will be cancelled for the remainder of the cruise.'

Loud groans echoed through the room as Lana bit back a grin. Sailor boy didn't have a clue how desperate a bunch of women out for their daily endorphin fix could be, and if he thought a simple apology would cut it, he was in for a big surprise.

Zac was speaking again. 'However, she'll be able to check your gym programs from tomorrow. She'll be here between ten and three, though purely in a supervisory role. Thanks for your understanding.'

His thanks were pre-emptive. No sooner had he finished speaking than angry women besieged him.

'You've got to be joking. I've saved for five years to take this cruise and that's it? No aerobic classes? I must do my classes every day.'

'When I pay for service I damn well expect it!'

'The ship's company will be hearing about this when I get off this ship.'

'Isn't there anyone else to take over?'

He held up his hands, the smile long gone in the face of this terry-towelling tirade. 'Ladies, please. If you'll give me a chance to—'

'Now, listen here, mister. This is my tenth cruise, and I've cruised with different shipping lines all over the world. So far the service on this ship stinks.'

A large woman crowbarred into a purple leotard stood toe to toe with Zac, hands planted on ample hips.

'Ever since I set foot on this tub things have gone wrong. The air-conditioning in my cabin didn't work, the balcony door jammed, the incompetent waiters mixed up my dinner, the dance instructor was called away at the last minute only to be replaced by the likes of *you*, and now this. What next?'

Another woman stepped forward, her rake-thin body clad in designer gear—the type you don't sweat in—her coiffed blonde hair far too perfect for such an early hour of the morning.

'I'm surprised, Mr McCoy. In my day a PR man knew how to handle life's little dramas such as this. In fact, he was paid to promote the delights of cruising. You, on the other hand, don't seem to be earning your wage at all. I would even say you're rather incompetent.'

Oh-oh. The situation had turned from tense to downright ugly in the space of two minutes, and Lana felt sorry for him, wanting to help but unwilling to interfere.

Before he could utter a word, the designer dame jabbed an accusatory finger in his direction. 'I presume you know who I am, Mr McCoy?'

He nodded, his lips set in a grim line but his confident aura firmly in place. Lana had glimpsed the same unflappable Zac last night, after the kiss, when she'd slammed her barriers back in place and taken her anger out on him.

'Not only do Mr Rock and I contribute handsomely to this particular shipping line, our personal recommendations go a long way to securing promotions for staff onboard. Personally, I'm having a hard time finding *any* worthy staff on this ship.'

She punctuated the air with short, sharp jabs of her hand, lending weight to every word.

'And, furthermore, I recommend you rectify this farce as soon as possible.'

She spun around and sailed out of the room like the *Queen Mary,* majestic, impressive, unstoppable.

Nobody deserved to be publicly berated like that and, taking in Zac's tense posture and clenched jaw, Lana felt for him.

She knew what it was like to be on the receiving end of criticism like that—had faced it eight weeks earlier, when she'd appealed to the museum's CEO to let her be the spokesperson on the Egypt trip.

The result? If her self-confidence hadn't been much to start with, it had been non-existent after that meeting, when he'd told her in no uncertain terms she wasn't 'the face the museum is looking for'.

Apparently she was too reserved, too serious, too conservative. All perfectly legitimate qualities in a head curator, but not good enough to front TV cameras and reporters at the digs of their newest discovery. That honour had gone to her trainee, a woman with a bigger mouth, bigger boobs and a bigger wardrobe than her.

It had hurt. A lot. A whole damn lot.

She was brilliant at her job; it was the one thing that made her feel good about herself. Little wonder her limited self-esteem had plummeted as a result, and she needed this trip to give it a boost in the right direction.

Battling the sting of bitter tears threatening to complete her humiliation that day in the CEO's office, she'd vowed to gain confidence and never be overlooked for a work opportunity again.

After that kiss last night she'd taken a huge backward step, retreat being her best form of defence.

But now she possessed skills to help Zac out. Maybe she could take another baby step forward? What better way than taking a class she'd been trained to do?

She taught at the museum all the time, instructed students and peers alike, and it was the only time she never felt self-conscious in front of a group. She enjoyed teaching, enjoyed imparting skills to others, so why not here, now?

Clenching and unclenching her hands several times, she shook them out, wishing she could shake off her nerves as easily.

Tension clawed at her tumbling tummy, and she inhaled in and out, long, slow breaths, to clear her head and give her clarity of thought.

Maybe not such a good idea, as the more she thought about it the more she wanted to bolt for the safety of her cabin. But hiding away wouldn't improve her confidence.

It was now or never.

With a last deep indrawn breath, she marched towards Zac. 'Could I have a word with you?'

He rubbed at the bridge of his nose as a low rumbling resumed through the gym. It was the first time he'd appeared faintly rattled. 'Now isn't the time.'

'I can help. I'm a qualified fitness instructor. I can take this class right now, if you want me to.'

'*You're* a fitness instructor?'

He made it sound as if she was a space cadet, and his assessing gaze swept over her. Yeah, as if her outfit made any difference to her credentials.

'You really want to do this?'

'I wouldn't have offered otherwise.'

Relief eased the tension in his face, his lips kicking into a mischievous grin. 'Does it mean I'll owe you?'

She almost ran at that point, the memory of that sexy smile seconds before he'd kissed her all too fresh as she focussed on his lips.

'You won't owe me a thing.'

'Oh, but I will.'

Heck, how had this turned from her doing him a favour to having him in her debt?

With that beguiling smile and heat smouldering in his eyes, she was floundering out of her depth more than ever.

'Look, just forget it—'

'Go ahead and take the class. Once you're done, drop by my office.'

He straightened, brisk and businesslike, and she wondered if she'd imagined the loaded exchange a moment ago.

'Okay.'

As she turned away he laid a hand on her arm. Her skin burned despite the innocuous touch.

'One more thing.'

'What's that?'

'Just so you know—I always pay my debts.' He paused, his disarming smile capable of tempting a saint. 'And I fully intend making good with you.'

While her tongue glued itself to the roof of her mouth, his eyes glittered with clear intent before he released her and walked away.

Lana tucked strands of frizz into her bristling ponytail, all too aware she was fighting a losing battle as she stared at her flushed face covered in a perspiration sheen. The polished brass nameplate on the door to Zac's office was as highly effective as a mirror—too effective—and she belatedly realised she should've ducked down to her cabin before presenting herself here.

When he'd said he'd see her after the class he wouldn't have anticipated a bedraggled, scraggly mess arriving at his office. Then again, it wasn't as if she was trying to impress him. The opposite, in fact. The sooner he realised he couldn't charm her like every other woman on the planet, the easier her life would be. Even if a small part of her would miss his banter.

She knocked and waited for a 'come in' before pushing the door open. The sight that greeted her snatched the breath from her lungs.

She'd seen his many faces—sailor Zac, resplendent in uniform, dancing Zac, dinner companion Zac—yet the sight of him behind a desk, scrawling across a daily planner with one hand, tapping a keyboard with the other, issuing instructions into a hands-free phone all the while, had her grabbing the door to steady her wobbly knees.

Here was a guy in control—a guy who could do anything he set his mind to. He made multi-tasking look easy, and when he glanced up and smiled a welcome she had to steel her resolve, for executive Zac was as appealing as the rest. More so, considering she understood work, thrived on work, her life was *all* work.

'I'll get back to you. In the meantime, make sure those timetables are correct to within a second.'

He stabbed at the disconnect button on the phone, threw his pen down and leaned back in his chair, hands clasped behind his head.

'Well, well—if it isn't our very own Jane Fonda.'

With a shrug, she crossed the room and plopped into a chair opposite him. 'Jane Fonda? Aren't you showing your age? Her exercise videos are years old.'

He laughed. 'So how did it go? Bet those women didn't give *you* a hard time.'

'Why would they? Besides, I think they took out all their frustrations on you.'

'Did they ever.'

He dropped his hands and stood, his sudden proximity

making her rethink her choice of seat. The wide, stuffy leather chair in front of his desk had seemed perfect while he was seated, but now, with him towering over her, it wasn't so appealing.

'Thanks for stepping in and saving my butt.'

Oh, no. She wouldn't think about his butt…wouldn't go there…wouldn't remember how she'd made a grab for it last night in that fit of insanity.

Grateful she could blame her flaming cheeks on exercise rather than embarrassment, she cleared her throat. 'You're welcome.'

'Now that you're here, it's time we had a chat.'

'About?'

His eyes bored into hers, challenging, determined, as he gestured towards a document on his desk.

'Your employment contract, of course.'

CHAPTER FIVE

'PARDON?'

She tapped her ear, just to make sure she'd heard correctly.

He picked up the document and offered it to her. 'Take a look. It's your employment contract.'

'You're kidding, right?'

She stared at the document as if it was her marching orders to walk the plank. 'I'm on holiday. A well-earned holiday, I might add. I helped you out of a tight spot back there, but that's it.'

He threw the contract back on the desk and perched on the desk in front of her—way too close for comfort.

'I understand how you feel, but I need your help. You'd only have to take two classes a day. In return, you'll be well paid, and it won't interfere with your holiday at all. You love your job, don't you?'

'My job?'

A puzzled frown knit his brow. 'You said you're a qualified fitness instructor?'

'I am.'

But that wasn't her job. Her job entailed wearing boring business suits, cataloguing boring artefacts and devising boring staff rosters.

Okay, so she did love her job, and it wasn't always dull, but after she'd been passed over for the Egypt trip she'd started craving more, needing more, and—strangely—the opportunity now came from the most unlikely source. She stared straight at him.

Right then, it hit her like a meteor from Mars.

She needed to build her confidence this trip, and wanted to try new things in order to do so, but still she felt stifled by her conservative nature.

So what if she stepped into a new role? Became the type of person she'd like to be if she had more nerve? Besides, it wasn't as if she was lying. She *was* a qualified aerobics instructor. She just didn't do it for a living.

And who knew? Maybe doing this would give her the ability to form a coherent answer without wanting to duck her head in embarrassment every time he smiled her way?

'Let me take a look at that.'

Trying to hide a triumphant grin and failing, he handed her the contract.

'I took the liberty of contacting Madigan Shipping, the company that owns the *Ocean Queen*. I explained the circumstances and they approved a temporary employment contract—particularly when they heard the Rocks were onboard. They're influential people in shipping circles.'

'Do you always organise other people's lives, or will I actually have a say in your grand plan?'

His grin broadened. 'You're here, aren't you? And I'm giving you the option to sign on or not.'

'Yeah, right.'

Skimming the contract, she nearly fainted when she spied the remuneration—on a par with her monthly salary.

For taking two lousy classes a day? Too easy. And there was that new futon she'd coveted for the spare bedroom in her flat. Not to mention the slight shoe fetish she'd developed thanks to Beth's cast-offs. This extra cash would come in mighty handy for a pair or two of her own.

'What do you think?'

'I think I'm nuts, but why not?'

She picked up the pen he'd discarded earlier and signed the contract. 'There.'

'Don't forget I owe you.'

His eyes glowed, magnetic and enticing, and she suppressed a shiver at what her payment might entail.

'Don't worry about it.' She tugged at her ponytail, twisting the ends around her finger in a nervous habit she'd had since childhood. 'This is turning into some holiday. The ship's amazing, the ports are interesting, and that kiss last night—'

She bit her tongue and mentally slapped herself for running off at the mouth and thinking out loud. That kiss was history, remember? Forgotten. Never happened.

His gaze focused on her mouth, and her lips tingled as his blistering stare remained riveted. Surreptitiously she scratched behind her ear, where her skin prickled the most.

What had happened to the woman who'd just instructed an aerobics class for the first time and nailed it? What had happened to her newfound bravado? It looked as if it had deserted her, along with her common sense. Imagine thinking she could sign on as an employee and keep her distance from Zac.

She fidgeted, shifting her weight from one foot to the other, then rubbed the nape of her neck, wound her hair around her finger.

His gaze finally lifted from her mouth, only to lock onto her eyes, and all that endless blue was enticing and intense. She looked away first and gestured to the desk.

'Don't you have work to do?'

'It can wait.'

She couldn't stand all this tension, the air practically crackling between them, and she backed towards the door. 'Well, I need a shower, so I'd better go.'

He stalked towards her, like a powerful alpha wolf shadowing a helpless, quivering rabbit.

'But what about working out what I owe you?'

She waved her hand, fluttering. It was ineffectual at keeping him at bay. 'The payment's all there in the contract. Clearly spelled out in black and white.'

Stopping less than a foot in front of her, he leaned forward and she gasped.

'Nothing's ever that clear. There are many shades of grey here I think we need to figure out.'

Her breath caught as his head lowered, her heart pounding as if she'd just taken ten aerobics classes back to back.

'Like?'

It came out a squeak, and she darted a glance to the door handle a few inches from her hand. She should grab it, twist it, make a run for it. But she couldn't, was trapped beneath that disconcerting stare, overpowered by his sheer masculinity as he towered over her.

For one insane second she almost wished he'd kiss her again and get it over with, but instead he straightened, ran a hand through his hair and gestured towards his desk.

'Like a stack of paperwork, tax forms and so on that you need to fill out. How about you go take that shower and meet me back here in half an hour?'

She almost collapsed against the door in relief—or was that disappointment?

Buoyed by the fact she'd just had a lucky escape, she saluted. 'Aye-aye, sir.'

With her hand on the door handle, she couldn't resist a parting shot, considering he'd had the upper hand ever since she'd set foot in here.

'You know something? I'm looking forward to being your colleague. You might actually let up on me if we're co-workers.'

She closed the door as Zac sank into his chair and stared at the contract she'd signed, the fine print blurring.

Colleague.

Co-worker.

Lana Walker, the woman who was slowly but surely driving him crazy, was now his colleague, his co-worker, neatly circumventing his golden rule of never getting involved with a passenger.

Hell.

He leaned back and closed his eyes. It didn't help, as an instant image of pert breasts, narrow waist, toned abs and slim legs covered in Lycra haunted him. She wasn't tall, yet her perfect proportions gave the illusion of height—and he ached to touch her, every tempting inch.

Dammit, why couldn't she have stayed hidden behind those loose dresses and revolting pants she wore? First the wet one-piece and now this: tight candy-striped Lycra bike shorts, and a T-shirt fitted enough to highlight the curves he'd love to run his hands over.

He'd snuck back to the gym, watched the last few minutes of her class. And he had been blown away.

In a whirl of high kicks, arm twirls and jiggling breasts, she'd morphed from shy innocent to action goddess, and no matter how hard he tried he couldn't wipe her from his mind.

This teasing was getting out of hand. It had been fun at the start, amusing to get a smile out of that prim mouth, a rare fiery flash from those sombre hazel eyes. But somewhere along the way the lines had blurred, and what had started out as a bit of harmless fun to get a subdued woman to lighten up had morphed into his wanting her.

Seriously wanting her. His thoughts consumed by her day and night.

That kiss on the beach last night had changed everything.

He'd given in to temptation unprepared for the ferocity of her response—a response that had kept him up all night wishing he hadn't let her flee.

First her astounding response. Now her metamorphosis from shy and nervous to bouncy and brilliant.

If he hadn't been intrigued enough before, he sure as hell was now, and despite the importance of keeping his mind on the job this cruise, he had to know more.

What was it about her that had him coiled tighter than an anchor chain?

He rubbed the bridge of his nose, but it did little to erase the beginnings of a headache building behind his eyes.

She was forthright and tetchy—not his type at all. Yet she was so delightfully unaffected, with an underlying hint of vulnerability that tugged at his heartstrings no matter how hard he tried to ignore the fact he still had a heart.

But he couldn't get involved. At least not emotionally. Not now.

Besides, how would she feel if she knew he'd conned her? He hadn't placed any call to head office. He didn't have to. One of the perks of being the boss.

Speaking of which, he needed to get back to work. He was close, so close, to discovering the saboteur who was plaguing the company.

While Shelley's fall might well have been an accident, there had been a couple of other incidents that weren't as easily dismissed. His uncle's suspicions that the *Ocean*

Queen would be the next target had been well-founded. And the sooner he found the person who hadn't disclosed a reckless disregard for everyone's safety and comfort when boarding, the easier things would be for his uncle.

He owed Jimmy and, as he'd told Lana, he always paid his debts.

What would she think of the purely carnal payback system he'd like to instigate with her?

Lana stood under the shower, cool water sluicing down her body. She closed her eyes and tilted her head back, enjoying the spray peppering her face, though it did little to wash away the memory of that damn kiss.

She was determined to forget it, to relegate it to the back of her mind alongside other horrific moments, like the time she had walked in on one of her students with the museum taxidermist in a decidedly unstuffy moment in the archive room, or the time she'd bawled when she'd got her first promotion.

Truly shuddery, forgettable moments—just like her response to that kiss last night.

So why couldn't she wipe the memory, however hard she tried?

As she tipped her head forward and tied a towel turban-style around her dripping hair, she had a vision of Zac's hungry stare as she'd left his office. Not that she'd wanted to provoke him—far from it. But he delighted in rattling her, in teasing her, and she'd wanted to get one back.

It hadn't worked. The desire in his gaze had been real, potent, and oh-so-scary for a novice like her. Old Lana would have jumped ship and swum back to shore before he could wink. But she wasn't the old Lana any more.

The old Lana wanted a husband, a family, a house in the

suburbs to come home to every night after another satis-
fying day at the museum.

The new Lana still wanted all those things, but for the
first time in her life she was experiencing the flicker of excitement that came with self-assurance—the heady rush of
having a guy like Zac pay attention to a geek like her.

She'd never had that. Jax had faked a few compliments,
fuelled her need to be noticed by a guy—any guy—and had
reeled her in as part of his plan. He had used her before
saying she was frigid when she couldn't deliver what he'd
wanted. His disdain haunted her to this day.

She knew his accusation was why she didn't date very
often, why she froze when a guy got physically close.

So why had she combusted in Zac's arms during that kiss?

Subconsciously she knew.

She wanted to feel alive, wanted to tap into the passion
simmering deep inside, wanted to be bold and brazen and
beautiful rather than a mousy, boring workaholic.

Zac had a way of looking at her as if she was the only
woman in the world, and when he did the small, wistful part
of her that wanted to be that confident woman dared to hope.

She made it back to his office with a minute to spare.

'Come on in. I've got the forms for you.'

'Great.'

As she stepped into the office he briefly touched her
elbow, bending lower on the pretext of closing the door.
'What? No perfume?'

Her gaze snapped to his, only to catch a fleeting
glimpse of a cheeky grin before he turned away. Her scowl
was wasted.

'Why don't I take them away with me, fill them out, and
drop them at the front desk when I'm done?'

She might be feeling braver after breezing through the class, but there was something about him now—the way he looked at her, as if seeing her in a new light. While she should be happy, her inner introvert trembled at what he might do if he sensed the change in her.

He tapped the stack on his desk, beckoned her over. 'Believe me, when you take a look at these you'll be thanking me for filling them out here. I've helped employees through the rigmarole before; we'll get it done in half the time.'

Okay, so he was being helpful. Then why did it feel like the Big Bad Wolf lending Red Riding Hood a hand before gobbling her up?

'Right—let's get to work, then.'

She plopped on the chair opposite his, drew the forms towards her.

He stilled her hand by placing his on top, setting her pulse racing as she stifled the urge to yank her hand away.

'Not much intimidates you, does it?'

She raised an eyebrow. If he had any idea how her heart thumped, her lungs seized and her insides quaked at his simple touch, he'd withdraw that statement.

'I can usually handle stuff.'

Professionally, that was. Anything else and she was about as poised as a toddler on ice-skates.

'Think you can handle me?'

His voice had dropped seductively low, and the smouldering flame in his eyes warmed her, warning her that she was in way over her head with this one if she thought for one second a small boost in confidence could cope with the likes of him at his tempting best.

'I'm sure it wouldn't be too hard.'

She almost bit her tongue in frustration, unwittingly adding to the wordplay. Heat suffused her cheeks, and she wished she had the guts to toss her hair over her shoulder, not duck her head like the blushing virgin she almost was.

His grin had tension strumming her taut muscles. 'You're very assured when you want to be.'

Only when he needled her enough that she forgot her shyness.

'Mainly when putting guys like you back in your place.'

He leaned forward, close enough to whisper in her ear. 'Guys like me?'

Resisting the urge to jerk back from his proximity, she settled for a subtle slide of her hand out from under his instead.

'Over-confident. Smooth. Charming. Used to getting your own way.'

Rather than being offended, he laughed. 'Guilty as charged.'

He leaned into her personal space again, crowding her, overwhelming her, confusing her.

'So, is it working?'

'What?'

'My charm.'

'Not a bit.'

She crossed her fingers behind her back at the little white lie. 'Now, if there's nothing else, let's get these forms done so I can enjoy my holiday.'

'Actually, there was something else. You know I owe you?'

'Uh-huh.'

The instant wariness in Lana's eyes made Zac chuckle.

'How about a tour when we dock in Suva? I've got the day off, so I could show you the sights. What do you think?'

Her eyes lost their cautious edge as her lips curved into a smile—the type of genuinely happy smile that could easily tempt a man to want more, a lot more.

'Sounds good. Know any hot spots?'

Yeah. Just below her ear, above her collarbone, and dead on her soft lips…

'Several.'

His tone must have alerted her to his thoughts, for her eyes widened, glowed with understanding, till he could distinguish the tiniest green flecks in the molten caramel before the shutters quickly descended.

'A tour sounds great.'

She dropped her gaze in record time, her tongue darting out to moisten her top lip. The nervous action did little to dissipate his growing interest in discovering what really made this tantalising woman tick.

Considering how much he wanted to get to know her, perhaps he should rethink Suva—especially his idea about taking her to his favourite secluded beach. If he could barely keep his hands off her here, what hope did he have in blissful isolation on the most spectacular stretch of pristine sand he'd ever seen?

'Right, it's a plan.'

He'd almost said a date, but dates implied more of that physical stuff he was afraid would scare her off. No matter how hard he tried, he couldn't wipe a vivid fantasy of the two of them splashing in the lagoon, him play-wrestling her, her wrapping her legs around him, her wet skin plastered to his, no clothes…

She stood abruptly, the chair almost toppling. 'Look, I really appreciate the offer to help, but I'll be fine with these forms. I'll holler if I need anything.'

Judging by her shaky voice she knew exactly what he was thinking, and she reacted the way she usually did: by erecting verbal barriers and making a run for it.

She scooped up the papers and made a dash for the door

in an awful fluorescent flurry of floral ankle-length skirt the colour of a lifejacket. Her hurried departure left him shaking his head as she slammed the door.

After she'd left, he sank into his chair and wiped a hand over his face. No—didn't help. He could still see her wide-eyed guarded expression, the hint of suspicion in those hazel depths, the wary curve of her lips.

She didn't trust him—didn't accept his interest as real. Not that he blamed her. He'd given her no indication to the contrary, playing the flirt, keeping things light-hearted, seeing how far he could push her before she reacted.

Someone or something had destroyed her belief in her attractiveness, and he'd hazard a guess that some jerk had done a number on her. It would explain her naivety, her lack of artifice when it came to playing coy or flirting back. Which meant he should give her a wide berth. Instead, he wanted her with a staggering fierceness, and the depth of his need was obliterating every common sense reason why he shouldn't do this.

He didn't need the distraction. He had a job to do. But if his head kept spinning like a compass needle his concentration would be shot anyway so maybe he should spend a bit of time getting to know her—the real her, not the cagey woman who hid her mistrust behind lowered eyes and fiddling hands.

Muttering a few curses which wouldn't make many of his colleagues blush, he picked up the phone and placed his daily call to Jimmy.

The phone rang three times precisely—the same number every day—which proved his uncle waited by the phone, despite his protests to the contrary that he totally trusted him that the company was in safe hands.

'Hey, Uncle Jimmy, it's me.'

'Zachary, my boy. How's things?'

Where should he start? With the part where he still felt like a fraud, running the company from behind the scenes until their culprit was caught, or the part where he was crazy for a woman who bolted every time he got close?

'Fine. I'm making progress.'

He didn't need to spell it out. His uncle had been the first to notice the ever-increasing number of 'accidents', the first to see the bad publicity begin to affect sales, and the one to notice the pattern of the incidents and predict the *Ocean Queen* would be next.

And, though he'd never admit it, the ensuing stress hadn't helped his battle with the illness that was slowly but surely killing him.

'Good. Because once you sort out the Australian side of things, there's that Mediterranean problem that needs attention.'

'All under control.'

He'd decided to run things from the London office for a year. More to do with the old man needing him there rather than with business. Not that Jimmy wanted to be mollycoddled. He'd made that perfectly clear. But under all that gruffness was a scared man fighting to stay alive, and Zac would be damned if he left the only father he'd ever known alone at a time like this.

He wanted to ask Jimmy how he was feeling, how the treatment was going, but knew he'd get the usual brush-off.

'So how's things in London?'

'All good here.'

He heard the strain beneath the forced upbeat tone.

'And you? How're *you* feeling?'

A slight pause followed by a grim throat-clearing. 'Can't complain.'

James Madigan wouldn't. He hadn't complained when Zac had left him in the lurch for a year, after he'd run off to marry Magda, hadn't complained when he'd had a near-fatal heart attack as a result of the stress from his increased workload—picking up the slack because of Zac's selfishness—and hadn't complained when Zac had outlined his plans for a future in direct opposition to his.

He was that sort of man: rock-solid, steadfast. And he was the man Zac owed everything to—the type of man he aspired to be.

'Your PR stint working out okay?'

'Yeah, the staff are buying it, and I'm getting the info I need, so that's the main thing.'

Jimmy coughed—an ear-splitting, hacking cough that chilled Zac's blood. Aware that his uncle hated appearing weak in any way, he quickly tried to distract him.

'Get this. I had Helena Rock on my case this morning, going berserk. Can't tell you how close I was to telling her I actually run the company now. That would've put the old battle-axe back in her place.'

Jimmy chuckled—something Zac wished he could hear more often. 'Lucky you didn't. Otherwise you'd have had a mutiny on your hands. Imagine if everyone knew I'd made you head honcho and hadn't announced it officially yet? You wouldn't get to catch the bastard hurting our ships, for a start.'

'You're right. But I hate lying. The staff respect and trust me as a fellow employee. I feel like I'm using them.'

'Don't be ridiculous. This is business. Cruise lines are becoming more competitive every day. We can't afford to let this stuff continue or it'll really start to hurt us. It's your company now.' He paused, the rattle in his throat indicating another cough coming on. 'I'd do the job if I could.

Unfortunately, I'm just an old sea dog who has to live vicariously through you these days, so make sure you do a damn good job.'

Zac searched for words to reassure him, to explain he couldn't be prouder that Jimmy was leaving him the company he'd built from scratch. Though he was glad to get a chance to feel the salt air in his face one last time.

As if reading his mind, Jimmy said the right thing—as usual.

'I wouldn't have placed you in charge of my empire unless I thought you were capable, Zachary.'

'Yeah—a regular shipping magnate, that's me.'

He'd wondered why his uncle had pushed him into shipping after he finished his commerce degree, not twigging that the crafty codger was grooming him till a year into his first contract. By then he'd been hooked—addicted to the shifting deck under his feet and the tang of salt air in his lungs.

He was proud to be in charge of the Madigan Shipping conglomerate, and would do whatever it took to make it the best damn shipping line in the world. He had big shoes to fill. He owed Jimmy. Now more than ever.

'You're doing a fine job, my boy. Now, you better get back to work. Just because you're the boss now, doesn't mean you can slack off.'

Zac laughed, half raising his hand in a salute just as he'd used to when he was a little boy, before dropping it uselessly, all too aware he wouldn't have much time left to share a joke with his uncle.

'You look after yourself.'

He only just heard a mumbled, 'You're as bad as these damn nurses,' before Jimmy hung up.

Life was short. Seeing a strong, vibrant man like Jimmy

fade away reinforced that, and he'd be damned if he sat here and let Lana disembark next week without fully exploring this unrelenting attraction driving him to seek her out almost every second of the day.

He didn't want to look back on this time and regret it—didn't want to be left with memories of a kiss and little else.

She could run but she couldn't hide, and tonight he'd make sure she knew exactly how much he wanted her.

A woman like Lana needed to be wooed, deserved to be treated right—starting with a romantic first date designed to bring a smile to her face and banish her doubts that he was anything other than genuine—in his pursuit of her, at least.

CHAPTER SIX

SHE was lousy at this.

Zac had flirted with her over starter, main course and dessert, showering her with flattery, teasing her, making her laugh. By the time she'd finished a divine lime tart smothered in lashings of double cream her sides and her cheeks ached, and he'd well and truly slipped under her guard despite logic telling her he was playing a game.

'Fancy having coffee in one of the lounges?'

He leaned towards her, immediately creating an intimacy excluding the rest of the people at their table. It set her pulse racing, throwing her off balance quicker than the two-metre swells buffeting the ship.

'Only if you let up with the compliments.'

'Why?'

His eyes darkened like storm clouds scudding across a midnight sky.

'It's overkill.'

'But all true.'

She raised an eyebrow and sent a pointed look at her un-adorned navy shift dress. 'You think I look good in this?'

His gaze dipped to her dress, lifted to focus on her lips, before his curved into a roguish smile.

'What you wear is irrelevant. You're beautiful.'

She exhaled on a soft sigh, wishing for one incredible moment she could be seduced into believing him, giving in to his low voice, his hypnotic eyes, his sincere expression. But she wasn't beautiful, far from it, and falling under a suave sailor's spell was beyond foolish.

'Now that you've exercised all those smooth sailor boy lines for the evening, maybe I will have that coffee. I'm in need of a caffeine hit to wake me from the stupor you've got me in after all that stuff you've been shovelling.'

He laughed. 'It's a date. Just let me drop by the office to check on a fax, and I'll meet you in the Crow's Nest Lounge in ten minutes?'

'Make it five?'

'Can't bear to be away from me for long?'

'Actually, I was thinking more of the fact I need to be up early for my first official aerobics class, so I don't want to be out too late.'

'Spoilsport. I thought you might be pumping up my ego for a delusional moment there.'

'Like you need it.'

Tapping her watch face, she sent him a saccharine-sweet smile. 'Four minutes and counting. If you want that coffee you'd better get a move on.'

He held up three fingers. 'Bet I beat you there.'

'You're on.'

She made a dash for the Ladies' on the way, unable to resist touching up her lipstick. Woeful behaviour for a girl who rarely wore anything but a slick of moisturiser back home, but considering he kept studying her as if she was a priceless painting she had no choice. That sort of scrutiny put a girl under pressure—especially one who didn't feel

beautiful, let alone believe she deserved compliments—
and she needed all the help she could get.

As she strolled into the Crow's Nest with ten seconds
to spare, her stomach somersaulted as she caught sight of
Zac at a cosy table for two in the farthest corner, beckon-
ing her over with a smug smile.

'What did you do? Sprint the whole way?'

He pulled out a seat for her and she sank into it before
her knees gave the telltale wobble they had whenever he
got too close.

'The fax hadn't arrived. I ducked my head in the door,
had a quick look, and headed straight here. What about
you? Have a quick dip overboard before you joined me?'

She tilted her nose in the air and sent him a withering
stare. 'First I'm beautiful; now I look like a drowned rat.
You need to work on your charm.'

'That's what you're here for.' He trailed a fingertip down
her forearm and her breath caught. 'I need the practice.
Now, fancy a coffee? Drink?'

'Make mine a double,' she muttered, snatching her arm
away and sending him a disapproving glare that did little
to curb his sexy smile.

'Really?'

She waved him away. 'No, just order me something
sweet and yummy.'

'You've already got it. But I'll get you a drink too.'

Poking her tongue out in response to his corny
comeback, she waited till he'd headed for the bar before
grabbing a coaster and fanning her face.

Every second she spent in his company was confusing
her further. The closest she'd come to feeling like this
before was watching *Ocean's Eleven*. What hope did a girl

have with George Clooney, Brad Pitt and Matt Damon on screen simultaneously?

She'd only agreed to Zac's invitation because she didn't want to head back to her tiny cabin just yet—didn't want to be alone.

Tonight was the anniversary of Jax spitting the truth at her—the anniversary of the night he'd dumped her in no uncertain terms. And while she'd made a new life, moved to a new city, taken up new activities, she couldn't forget the devastation, the embarrassment that she'd made such a monumental error in judgment.

It wasn't a night to be alone. It was a night to be distracted with funny quips and compliments, no matter how meaningless, a night to erase the memories of how naïve she'd once been.

'You okay?'

Her heart sank as he dumped their drinks on the table and pulled his chair next to hers, concern creasing his brow.

Blinking rapidly, she pointed to her contact lens. 'Still not used to these darn things. Wish I'd brought my glasses this trip.'

His eyes narrowed as they locked onto hers, probing, yet compassionate. 'I'd believe you if I hadn't seen your expression.' He jerked his thumb over his shoulder towards the bar. 'From over there you looked like someone had died. Then I get back here and you're almost crying—'

'I'm not!'

She sniffed as a lone tear chose that moment to squeeze out of her eye and roll down her cheek, plopping on the back of her hand clenched in her lap.

'The hell you're not.' He brushed a thumb under her eye, so tenderly she almost burst into tears on the spot. 'Now why don't you tell me what's really going on?'

She shook her head, mortified he'd seen her like this, frantically racking her brain for something halfway plausible to tell him—anything other than the truth.

Placing his hand over hers, he gave it an encouraging squeeze. 'Tell me.'

She opened her mouth, closed it, then repeated her goldfish impersonation. Her mind was blank apart from the glaring truth: that it had been over three years since Jax had dumped her, and the memory still had the power to make her blubber.

'It's a guy, isn't it? What did the jerk do?'

Her gaze focussed on his, her tears rapidly drying under all that fierce, fiery blue. He almost looked possessive, protective, and she found herself wanting to tell him. A small part of her was thrilled he actually seemed to care.

'Tonight's an anniversary of sorts.'

She stared down at his hand covering hers: tanned, strong, oh, so comforting. Some of that strength transferred to her as she took a deep breath and kept talking.

'I loved this guy—thought he was the one. He said all the right things, did all the right things, but turned out he was only after…one thing.'

She'd almost blurted the truth—that Jax had only been schmoozing her for what she could do for him at the museum. He'd wanted insider info on items for his private collection. But she couldn't tell Zac about any of that, considering he thought she was a fitness instructor.

'We didn't really click, so he dumped me.' She shrugged, hating the lance of pain still lodged deep in her heart. 'Said I was just a fling, a bit of fun.'

She hiccupped, a pathetic half-sob, angry at the sting of yet more tears, angry at herself more for being such a gullible fool.

'He laughed at me for getting so involved, for being old-fashioned and taking our relationship seriously.'

Zac cursed under his breath, turning his hand over to intertwine his fingers with hers. 'You listen to me. That piece of slime didn't deserve you. He isn't worth anything let alone you giving him a second thought.'

'I know.'

She sighed, enjoying the secure feeling of her fingers intertwined with his way too much. Holding her hand was a fleeting, comforting gesture—something a guy like him would do for any woman. But for one tiny moment it made her feel beyond special, as if he really cared.

'Come with me.'

He leaped to his feet, practically dragging her with him.

'But what about our drinks?'

'Forget them. Let's go.'

'Where?'

She had to almost run to keep up with him. His long strides were determined.

'Somewhere I should've taken you first, rather than easing into this date with a drink.'

Her jaw hit the deck as he pushed through a heavy glass door and led her out onto the open promenade. 'Date?'

'Yeah, date. You know—that thing two people do when they want to get to know each other better, when they like each other even if one of them doesn't want to admit it.'

If her mind had spun with memories of Jax, it was positively reeling now with Zac's little announcement.

They reached the railing and he finally released her hand, leaned forward, his gaze fixed on the undulating ocean. 'I've gone about this all wrong. I didn't want to scare you off by calling this a date tonight, but I'd planned on bringing you up here, talking a little, getting to know each other, before catching a movie or maybe going dancing—or whatever you wanted to do.'

'Oh.'

She couldn't speak, the pain of memories of Jax annihilated by the unbelievable joy unfurling in her heart.

He turned to face her, reached over and stroked her cheek, soft, beguiling. She held her breath, stunned by his intimate touch, and by her craving for more.

'I wanted tonight to be romantic, to show you I'm not just toying with you.'

He stepped closer, took hold of her arms, and she looked up, gasped, captivated by the moonlight glinting off his dark curls and the striking shadows it created as it played across his face.

He slid his hands up and down her arms, the rhythmic contact depriving her of all rational thought as he gazed at her with hunger and greed and passion.

'I don't know what to say—'

'Then don't say anything at all.'

He tugged her close a second before crushing her lips beneath his. The scorching kiss, a sensual assault, left her reeling.

If their first kiss on the beach in Noumea had rocked her world, this kiss blew it into the stratosphere.

As she tilted, along with the deck beneath her shaky feet, she realised she'd never been kissed like this—ever.

She clung to him as his tongue coaxed its way into her mouth, teasing her to match him. She moaned, a guttural sound deep in her throat, and the noise inflamed him. He leaned into her, pressing her back against the rail as his arousal strained against her, creating an answering response in her core, setting her wildest desires alight.

She should stop this madness, re-erect the barriers that

had come crashing down the first instant his lips had touched hers.

But it felt so good to be desired, so good to have the attention of a man, so good to eradicate any lingering memories of what had happened on this night three years ago.

His hands tangled in her hair, angling her head, and he slid his lips repeatedly across hers as he tried to pull her closer.

Stunned by the ferocity of his need, she inadvertently rotated her hips against his pelvis as his hand strayed to her breast, cupping and kneading, sending her resistance spiralling dangerously out of control. His thumb circled her nipple through the thick cotton of her dress, the torturous rubbing firing electric shocks through her body.

The sound of a slamming door broke the erotic spell and they tore apart. Her breathing was ragged as he ran a hand through his mussed curls, his expression dazed.

She'd lost control in his arms—and she never, ever lost control. She was the epitome of control at work.

Christmas parties? She'd be the sober one, tidying up after everyone left.

Farewelling staff? She'd do the collection and choose the perfect gift.

Organising holiday rosters? All over it.

All over Zac, more like it. Her famed control was washed away on the tide.

He laid a tentative hand on her shoulder. 'Lana?'

'Hmm?'

She didn't know what to say, didn't know where to look. Focussing on Beth's indigo pumps with the gold wedge heel seemed a good start.

He tipped her chin up, leaving her no option but to meet his gaze. 'I have absolutely no control around you.'

She laughed—a brittle sound whipped away by the wind. 'I was just thinking about control.'

His hand hesitated, his thumb brushing her jaw before he dropped it. 'My lack of it?'

'Mine, actually.'

She hadn't wanted him to kiss her, hadn't wanted him to remind her of how good it had been the first time, but since he had, she was glad. Glad he'd made her feel desirable and womanly and special for an all too brief moment.

'You don't have to say anything. You were trying to cheer me up. I get it.'

He let another expletive rip. 'If you think that was a pity kiss, you're out of your mind.'

Out of her mind, all right. Out of her mind with wanting him to do it again and again and again.

'It wasn't?'

Shaking his head, he cradled her face, forcing her to look him in the eyes. 'You have no idea what you do to me.'

Flicking her tongue out to dampen her swollen lips, she said, 'I think I have some idea.'

Her wry response garnered a smile. 'I thought you were immune to my charm?'

'There's no vaccination strong enough against you, it seems.'

They grinned at each other like a couple of starstruck adolescents, the brisk ocean breeze buffeting them, pushing her towards him in an act from the heavens.

She'd usually flee—find a quiet place and dwell on why he kept chasing her when she wasn't remotely chaseworthy.

Though she didn't run at work; there she solved problems, enjoyed the challenge. Just ask her colleagues where she could be found: at the museum at all hours, tracking down the newest discovery, ensuring the latest display was eye-catching, cataloguing the backlog no one else wanted to do.

Thinking of the museum did it: she wasn't some *femme fatale* who went around inviting kisses from charming sailors on a moonlit night. She was career-focussed, with an aim to reach the top of her field with a little more confidence. She should know better than to read anything into a few casual kisses and his wanting to *date* her—whatever that meant.

She might be inexperienced with men, but she was old enough to understand the purely chemical reaction when two people remotely attracted to each other flirted a little and that flirtation got out of hand.

'You're driving me to distraction.' He ran a hand through his hair for the second time in as many minutes, more rattled than she'd ever seen him. 'And, considering the job I have to do this trip, I can't afford any distraction.'

'And you're telling me this because…?'

He leaned forward, wound a strand of her hair around his forefinger and tugged gently. 'Because, despite every logical reason why I shouldn't do this, I'm struggling to keep my hands off you.'

'Oh.'

The wine she'd consumed at dinner sloshed around her stomach, rocking and rolling in time with her pounding heart as he tugged harder, bringing her lips centimetres from his before brushing a soft, barely-there kiss across her mouth. It was a tender kiss, at complete odds with the passionate exploding kisses they'd previously shared, a heart-rending kiss that reached down to her soul despite her intentions to ward it off.

When they broke apart she couldn't fathom the expression on his face, the shifting shadows in his eyes.

'I have to go check on that fax.'

'Right.'

'Stay out of trouble.'

With a brief touch on her cheek he was gone, leaving her thoroughly confused.

Within the space of an hour he'd comforted her, kissed her, and apparently dated her.

And what was that 'trouble' crack about? She'd never been in trouble in her life: the model student who studied hard and didn't party, the diligent worker first in of a morning, last to lock up at night. Good old dependable Lana. Reliable, steadfast, earnest Lana. Which was exactly why she was here, trying to build her self-esteem and convince herself a sexy sailor could just be the way to go about it.

He'd been nothing but honest about wanting her, so why the sudden scram? One minute his kiss had been warm and gentle and caring, the next he'd made a run for it.

Ironic, considering she hadn't run for once. She'd embraced her newfound bravery and stayed, even after that scintillating kiss that normally would have sent her scurrying for cover.

But she was done with running.

If she couldn't handle a healthy dose of honesty—something he'd just given her, even if the truth of how much he wanted her scared the hell out of her—how could she hope to become the poised, confident woman she needed to be at work?

She mightn't be able to give him what he wanted—would probably disappoint him if she did—but that didn't mean she couldn't lighten up a bit and actually enjoy his attention.

If she was really brave, she might even have a little fun along the way.

CHAPTER SEVEN

LANA spied Zac at the end of the gangway and sighed in relief. After he'd run out on her last night she'd had her doubts about him showing up today. Crazy, considering she was the one who'd usually contemplate a no-show rather than worrying about him doing it.

Beyond impressive in uniform, today he was casually cool in black board shorts, a funky printed T-shirt and a peaked cap, with aviator sunglasses shading his eyes. She wished she could see those eyes, read them, get a feel for his mood after last night.

She hadn't heard from him, hadn't seen him this morning, and while she was relieved, a small part of her couldn't help but wonder what he had planned for today.

If last night's 'date' hadn't exactly happened, maybe he had other ideas today?

Taking a deep breath, she headed down the gangway, half of her looking forward to the tour of Suva, the other half looking forward to seeing how far her confidence extended.

'I thought you'd stood me up.'

Tipping her head forward, she looked at him over the top of her sunglasses. 'Why would I do that? I've been looking forward to your tour.'

'I'm very good, you know.'

'Ever heard the phrase "self-praise is no praise"?'

He grinned and gestured to a small four-wheel drive parked nearby. 'Come on, I have a car waiting for us.' He bowed low. 'Your chariot awaits, madam.' He pulled off his cap with a flourish.

'*You're* going to drive?'

She glanced at the chaotic scene on the dock, where cars darted between pedestrians and street vendors, and horns honked constantly as people jumped out of the way of moving vehicles in haphazard fashion.

He laughed at her horrified, sceptical expression. 'Don't worry, I've done this before. The car belongs to Raj, a friend of mine. He often lends it to me if I want to tour around. Once we leave the docks and head out of town the roads quieten considerably.'

Her doubt must have shown, for his grin widened. 'Don't you trust me?'

She quirked an eyebrow. 'Your driving skills? Maybe. As for the rest? Not on your life.'

He clutched his heart. 'You're a hard woman. Now, come on—get in the car before I change my mind.'

She laughed, surprisingly relaxed as they headed out of town and he pointed out interesting landmarks.

She'd expected some awkwardness, but he kept up a steady flow of casual chatter as they wound around the island. Content to sit back and watch the stunning scenery, she admired the sapphire ocean lapping at pearly sands, the beaches fringed by swaying palm trees. After half an hour, they stopped at a roadside café.

'Do you like Indian food?'

'Love it. The hotter the better.'

'Good. Raj put me on to this place years ago, and I

always drop in if I have time. They make the best chicken tikka this side of India.'

'What are we waiting for? I'm ravenous.'

As they entered the open-air café the proprietor, a tall Sikh wearing a maroon turban, rushed over. 'Hello, Mr Zac. Welcome back.' He pumped Zac's hand so vigorously Lana feared the action might dislodge his turban. 'Aah, you have brought a beautiful friend. Welcome to Sujit's Place, miss.'

Zac smiled. 'Sujit, meet Lana.'

He bowed over her hand. 'Welcome. Now, what can I get you?'

She deferred to Zac. 'You order. You'd know the specialities.'

'How about the usual, Sujit?'

Sujit bowed again. 'Most definitely, my friend. Coming right away.'

She looked around, surprised by how clean the place was, considering it was open to the elements. As for the sand floor—it would be a breeze for clean-ups.

'Adds to the island ambience, huh?'

She nodded, surprised he could read her thoughts so easily, and secretly pleased. 'What's with the lack of table settings?'

'Wait and see.'

'Very mysterious.'

His mouth kicked up into a cheeky grin. 'All will be revealed shortly.'

'I bet.'

He chuckled at her laconic response and gestured to a nearby table, where she plonked her straw carryall next to a chair and sat, savouring the spicy aromas coming from the nearby kitchen.

'Smells divine.'

Zac slid his aviators off, the impact of all that dazzling

blue rivalling the sky for vibrancy. 'The last ship I was on used to dock here every week. I put on six pounds as a result. See?'

He lifted his shirt and patted his washboard stomach. Her mouth went dry. Those were some abs.

Before she had time to comment Sujit arrived, bearing platters of food: naan bread, chicken tikka, dahl and lamb korma were placed in a tantalising array in front of them, and the dryness disappeared as the delicious aromas made her mouth water.

'Thanks, Sujit. This looks superb, as always.'

Sujit nodded, his hands held together in a prayer-like pose. 'Enjoy your meal.'

Zac glanced at her, a smile playing about his lips. 'Well, what are you waiting for?'

Confused, she pointed at the table. 'Plates would be handy?'

'See those large green leaves Sujit put in front of us? They're not placemats; that's your plate. Indian food here is served on a banana leaf. Usually, only vegetarian fare is served on leaves, but here it saves on the washing up. You just roll them up once you've finished and throw them out. As for cutlery—you're looking at it.'

He waved his fingers at her, and she couldn't help but notice how long, elegant and strong they were.

'I can cope with using my hands to eat as long as I clean up first. Is that sink over there for washing?'

He nodded. 'Follow me.'

As they soaped and scrubbed his hand brushed hers and she jumped, the innocuous touch raising an awareness she'd determinedly subdued since last night.

He stared at her, an eyebrow raised, and she managed a weak smile. 'I think our food's getting cold.'

First to break the stare, she turned away, feeling hot and clammy and out of her depth. He'd moved the boundaries with those kisses, had changed everything with his admission of how much he wanted her, and no matter how hard she pretended she could handle it, she couldn't cast off all her reservations at once.

With her head urging her to take a chance for once, and her heart scared of the consequences if she did, she headed back to the table.

This was going to be a long day.

Zac followed Lana back to the table, loving how she moved, all fluid lines and sinuous elegance.

Her long turquoise dress, surely a reject from the seventies, flowed from her shoulders to mid-calf, skimming curves along the way. He could see the straps of a bright pink bikini poking through, and he hardened immediately at the thought of seeing her in it. If the vision of her hot little bod in that dreadful neck-to-toe one-piece had been haunting his dreams, he could hardly wait to see her curves revealed in a bikini.

She'd pulled her curly hair back in a loose ponytail, and he longed to reach out and wrap the tendrils that curled at the base of her neck around his fingers. He loved her hair, loved watching it bounce against her shoulders as she walked.

A vivid image of that hair draped over his torso popped into his mind and he almost stumbled. This would be one hell of a tour if he walked around with a hard-on all day.

Determined to ignore his libido, he sat and pushed a platter of naan towards her. 'Let's eat.'

'Everything looks delicious.'

'Wait till you try it.'

He ladled a serving of dahl and korma onto her leaf, then

reached for a naan. Her fingertips brushed his as he reached for the same piece and he clenched his jaw in frustration.

It wasn't deliberate—one look at her shy gaze firmly fixed on her banana leaf told him that—and he needed to get a grip before he made a mess of things, as he had last night.

He broke off a piece of the soft, doughy bread, dipped it into the pungent curry sauce and stuffed it into his mouth before he said something he'd regret, like, *Let's get out of here and get naked.'*

'Mmm, divine.'

Her tongue flicked out to capture a drip of sauce and he stifled a groan, focusing on the unique blend of spices hitting his tastebuds rather than how much he'd like to lick away that spillage.

He needed to talk, to draw attention away from how much he wanted her, to focus on anything other than the driving, obsessive need to get her naked and moaning his name while he plunged into her.

'Sujit whips up the best Indian food I've ever had. It rivals some of the feasts I've had in Singapore and India for authenticity.'

'You've been around, haven't you?'

'Yeah—definitely a perk of the job. I've travelled almost everywhere.'

'Any favourites?'

He'd steered the conversation onto safe ground only to be diverted by the small moans of pleasure she made between mouthfuls, and he gulped his entire glass of water before answering.

'Probably Alaska, for its glaciers. I've cruised the Inside Passage from Vancouver, and the ship usually spends a day in Glacier Bay. It's amazing that ships like ours, which weigh around seventy thousand tons, can sail to within a mile of those monsters. I've even seen huge chunks of ice sliding off the face.'

Maybe he should focus on that ice, focus on all that cold—anything to dampen the urge to leap across the table and drag her into his arms as she stared at him with wide-eyed awe.

'I also love the Mediterranean. Especially Italy. Capri is great, with its ancient cobbled streets and home-made pastas.'

He could have regaled her with tales of his travels all day, particularly as her wide, luminous eyes were fixed on him, her expression fascinated, but the longer she stared at him the harder it was to forget every sane reason why he couldn't push their involvement—no matter how much he wanted to.

He'd seen the devastation in her eyes last night, the lingering hurt from the jerk who had screwed her around, and her desolation at having their relationship labelled a fling.

He'd planned on backing away then, but once he'd taken her on deck, once he'd kissed her, his plans to leave her alone had drifted away on the night air.

He wouldn't hurt her by having a fling. But he couldn't offer her anything else, considering where he'd be for the next year. So where the hell did that leave them?

For now, he'd keep things light. He'd promised her a tour today—the least he could do after she'd come through for him with the exercise classes—and he'd make it a fun day for her if it killed him.

'You know, the South Pacific islands are growing in my favourite places ranking all the time.' He leaned forward and crooked a finger at her. 'I think the present company has a lot to do with that.'

She blinked, as if startled by his compliment, and he wished he could wring her ex's neck for battering her self-esteem to the point where she couldn't accept a compliment without embarrassment.

'You mean Sujit? I totally agree. His food is to die for. I haven't been to those other places, but I'd definitely put Fiji first on my list.'

He grinned at her clever sidestep, but he wasn't done yet. 'What about Noumea? How high should New Caledonia rate? I hear their moonlit beaches are magical.'

The recollection of their first kiss stained her cheeks pink. Her eyes dipped to her banana leaf as he belatedly remembered he was trying to cool down, not get more wound up.

She waved towards the food. 'You'll give me indigestion, flirting on an empty stomach. At least let me put a dent in this feast before you turn on the charm.'

He laughed, more relaxed than he'd been in years despite his desperate yearning for her. It had been that long since he'd enjoyed a woman's company enough to spend more than a few hours with her, and while he'd dated infrequently, he'd never experienced such a connection on so many levels with any woman. Not even Magda— and he'd married her.

'Let's finish up and hit the road. I can't wait to show you the island's best beach. It's isolated, so tourists haven't wrecked it.'

She mumbled an acknowledgement and focussed on her food. He wondered what he'd said. She'd been cool one moment, and perspiration covering her skin in a delectable sheen the next. A sheen that had him envisaging all sorts of erotic ways he could clean it off.

If he were prone to flights of fantasy he'd almost say she was hot and bothered about his mention of being on an isolated beach together. Yeah, and of course she wanted to rip his clothes off too. Definitely wishful thinking.

'Is the food too spicy for you?'

Her guarded gaze snapped to his, as if trying to read something into his innocuous question. 'No, it's fine. It's just a little hot today.'

Hot? It was positively burning—though the weather had little to do with it.

He gestured towards the kitchen, indicating drinks, and Sujit bustled out shortly after, bearing two tall, icy glasses and a pitcher.

'Ever had lassi before?'

'No.'

'It's made from yogurt. Very refreshing. It should cool you down a tad.'

While he'd need to dunk in a vat of the stuff to remotely cool down.

She took a tentative sip, before gulping the cold, sweet liquid and running the frosted glass across her forehead. Her eyelids fluttered shut as a relieved smile curved her lips. 'That was good.'

Okay, maybe the lassi had done the trick for her, but he was about to explode—and as she opened her eyes he bit back a groan.

'You've got a milk moustache. Here—let me.' He reached out before thinking better of touching her and pointed at her top lip, his words strangled.

She laughed and wiped her lip. 'Thanks. Not a good look.'

He smiled and stuffed another piece of naan into his mouth, concentrating on his food as he mopped up the last of his curry with the bread—anything to take his mind off how much he wanted her.

He topped up her glass and she drank again. He had the strongest urge to reach over, pull her head towards him and lick the lassi off her top lip.

Instead, he had to sit there and watch her do it, her

tongue flicking out to caress her lip in a slow sweep, and he almost bolted from the table.

'Finished? I'll take care of the bill and meet you at the car.'

She nodded, the loose strands of hair around her face floating in the breeze. The urge to brush them away made his gut clench all over again.

'Thanks for lunch. It was delicious. Sujit's a great cook.'

As he pulled out her chair, his hand brushed her bare arm, and he gritted his teeth at the feel of her silky, soft skin. At this rate he wouldn't be able to walk.

'See you at the car.'

Her open expression told him she had no idea how much he was struggling with his libido, and he turned away and called out to Sujit, who appeared from the kitchen in an instant.

'Mr Zac, your friend is special.' Sujit's singsong lilting accent held a wistful note. 'You have known her long, yes?'

'Not long. Though I agree she's special.'

So special he'd given up a valuable day to be with her. After last night he'd almost reneged on their tour; he could have spent the day catching up on paperwork and following up that fax pointing to their suspected saboteur.

But his wanting to cancel had been more than business; not only had that jerk of an ex done a number on her for sex, he'd lied to her—and the second Zac had heard that he'd known he shouldn't get involved.

He was lying to her too.

Every moment he let her believe he was a PR manager at sea he was being dishonest, and while catching the saboteur demanded duplicity—and ultimately making good on his promise to his uncle—it didn't stop him hating every second of his deceit.

So he'd told her a partial truth to compensate for his

guilt—told her how badly he wanted her, expecting her to run at the mention of a date let alone anything else.

Instead, her response to his kiss had shaken him as much as the fact that she'd stood her ground and hadn't run. And even while he'd planned on begging off the tour today the memories of her fiery reaction had kept him up all night and drawn him here.

'It must be serious. You have never brought a woman to Sujit's humble café before. Are you going to marry her?'

Zac laughed. Life was so simple in some cultures. You met a girl, you liked her, you married her. Either that or your parents chose a bride for you.

'No.' A strange tingle ran up his spine, causing the hairs on the back of his neck to stand on end. 'I'm just showing her around your lovely island today. She'll be leaving the ship in a week.'

'Ah, she lives in Australia. Why should that stop you from marrying? You also live there, yes?'

'Yeah, but she's a friend, and I'm not remotely interested in marrying her or anybody else for that matter.'

Been there, done that, never forgotten the folly.

Sujit grinned, his teeth stained an ugly brown from years of chewing betel nut. 'Whatever you say. Though trust old Sujit—he has a feeling in his bones about this one.'

'You're an old degenerate.' Zac settled the bill and shook his hand. 'See you next time.'

'Maybe you'll both visit on your honeymoon?'

Zac chuckled, amused by the restaurant owner's one-track mind.

Marriage again? Not for him.

As he caught sight of Lana, casually leaning against the Jeep, the wind whipping her hair away from her face while plastering the dated dress against her shapely body, the faintest niggle of doubt entered his mind.

She was dynamite, packing a stronger punch than TNT and C4 combined. She blew his mind and short-circuited the rest of his body every moment he spent with her, till all he could focus on was how much he wanted her.

He'd been attracted to her mentally at the start, but how quickly that had all changed. Now he wanted her so badly he ached.

Yet for all her surprising bravado last night she was still inherently shy, retreating when he pushed too far, still hiding her sensational body behind those repulsive clothes.

So if they couldn't have a fling, what the hell should he do? Back off?

'Mr Zac, I've never seen you like this.'

He tore his gaze away from Lana, focussed on Sujit. 'Like what?'

'Distracted.' Sujit pointed to his forehead, imitated a frown. 'So very serious.'

That's because his growing feelings for Lana were serious. Even the fact he was using the word 'feelings' scared the hell out of him.

Sujit shook his head, his benevolent grin bordering on condescending. 'I can see you're making this more complicated than it is. You like this woman, yes?'

He nodded, his gaze inadvertently drawn to her again. Crushing need swamped him, blindsiding him faster than a swinging mast.

'Well, then, do not over-analyse. Do not worry about the future and what it may hold. Live for the moment. See where the winds of change take you.'

He stared at Sujit as if seeing him for the first time, his words echoing through his head.

Could it really be that simple?

Was he over-analysing, thinking too far ahead, allowing his fears from the past to destroy a possible future with a wonderful woman?

His conscience yelled a resounding *Hell, yeah!* and just like that a mighty weight lifted from his shoulders and floated away into a cloudless Fijian sky.

'Thanks, my friend, you're a genius.' He pumped Sujit's hand, his attention still firmly focussed on the woman who'd captured his heart without trying.

Sujit's grin widened as he placed his palms together and bowed. 'I know. Now, go.'

He didn't need to be told twice, and as he headed for the car, refraining from breaking into a run, he knew the decision he'd just made had the potential to change his life. For the better.

Lana squinted into the sunshine, watching Zac stride towards the car. He'd been in a strange mood over lunch and the odd times she'd caught him staring at her it had looked as if he fancied her as dessert.

It had made her uncomfortable, and she'd had no idea how to handle the attention, so she'd focussed on her meal, steered the conversation onto factual topics and muddled through the best she could. She just hoped things weren't as tension-fraught at the beach.

'Ready to go?'

'Sure.'

As he drove along a winding coastal road she focused on the picturesque scenery and replayed their lunch conversation in her head.

There was so much more to him than smooth words and a charming smile. He was well-travelled, articulate and self-assured, with charisma that captured her interest and engaged her mind. It only added to his appeal. But she'd be better off remembering most of what he said was designed to tease her, that words were cheap.

She'd fallen for slick words before. These days a guy's actions were the only thing that would let him anywhere near her bruised heart.

'Wait till you check out this beach. I've seen a few, but I think this is better than some of the Caribbean beaches—not to mention Queensland's hot spots.'

'I love any beach. My apartment's in Coogee, so you can safely say I'm a bit of a beach babe.'

'Well, you're right about one thing. You're definitely a babe.'

Her measly ego inflated momentarily, before she shot him a disapproving stare. 'Oh, yeah, I'm sure my designer wardrobe elevates me to babe status.'

He paused, as if searching for the right words. 'Don't take this the wrong way, but your wardrobe is a little...'

'Boring?'

Her sour interruption had him darting a worried glance in her direction before refocusing on the road.

'I was thinking more along the lines of sedate for someone your age.'

'Which is?'

'Hell, I'm digging myself in deeper, aren't I?'

She chuckled. 'Quit while you're behind, sailor boy.'

She liked her clothes. They might be old but they were safe, familiar, like snuggling into a favourite quilt on a cold winter's day.

She'd tried a new wardrobe once before, a new look, going the whole way with risqué lingerie. But none of it had made any difference with Jax. He'd hurt her just the same, designer dresses or not. Much safer to stay true to herself, to find a man who wanted her for the real her, not because of how she looked or what she could do for him.

'Actually, I like what you're wearing today. That blue brings out the green flecks in your eyes.'

'My weird eyes change colour according to what I wear.'

'Not weird. How about alluring?'

She snorted. 'You could bottle that charm and sell it.' His bashful smile made her laugh. 'And I see what you mean. I'm so *alluring* I have *hundreds* of men falling at my feet, and it's all because of my eyes.'

'You have one.'

'Who?'

'I'm a male, in case you hadn't noticed.'

Oh, she'd noticed, all right—was noticing more by the minute, despite all attempts to the contrary.

Fortunately she was saved from replying as he slowed the car and turned into a narrow dirt track. The Jeep bumped and lurched over rough terrain, the ground scattered with large potholes, and thick foliage slapped against the doors.

Just as her bones started to warn her they'd been rattled once too often the vegetation thinned, and he pulled over into a clearing which overlooked an inviting stretch of white sand, with an aquamarine ocean that stretched as far as she could see.

'Wow—amazing.'

Zac's blue-eyed gaze fixed on her, bold, challenging. 'Sure is.'

He wasn't looking at the view, and she squirmed under his searing stare.

'Come with me.'

She stared at his outstretched hand, wanting to take it, but nervous he'd read too much into it.

He took the decision out of her hands by grabbing hers on the pretext of helping her from the car, and she sent him a tremulous smile, wondering if he had any idea what a big deal it was for her to hold hands with a gorgeous guy as they strolled towards a secluded beach.

Holding hands implied trust, implied dependence, implied she believed in him enough to lower her barriers—much more than responding to his impulsive kisses inspired by chemistry and the length of time since she'd last been kissed, and the soul-deep yearning to be wanted by another person.

As her feet sank into the soft sand, and he gripped her hand that little bit tighter, she knew her resistance to this charming man was slipping dangerously.

A loud 'caw' captured her attention, and she glanced to her right, at a huge bird perched on top of a towering cliff ending at the lagoon's edge.

That was exactly how she felt—as if she was standing on the edge of a very steep cliff, torn between wanting to jump into the warm, welcoming ocean below and experiencing the thrill of a lifetime, or letting her feet back her up to the predictable safety of solid ground.

With Zac tugging gently on her hand she had no option but to follow, heading into the unknown with a man who had the power to unnerve her, when every self-preservation instinct screamed at her to dig her heels in the sand.

CHAPTER EIGHT

'WELCOME to paradise."

They stopped beneath a coconut tree, the air fragrant with frangipani, the view picture-perfect.

'How did you find this place?' she whispered, reluctant to break the tranquility as they strolled towards the beach.

'Raj brought me here with his family. We had a picnic, swam in the lagoon, lazed around. It's great being able to relax away from the tourists swarming the island. I come back every chance I get, though I'm usually alone.'

'So you haven't brought a horde of women here before me?'

Though she kept her tone light, she knew some of her enjoyment would dissipate if he had brought countless others here.

He squeezed her hand. 'You're the first. I wouldn't share this place with just anyone.'

Oh-oh—there he went with more of that defence-shattering charm. With a nervous smile, she slipped her hand from his.

'More flattery. Aren't I the lucky one?'

He laughed. 'Come on, let's go for a swim.' He pointed to a row of palm trees. 'Let's dump our stuff over there. You get changed, I'll test the water.'

A great suggestion, as getting undressed in front of him would have made her beyond uncomfortable. Crazy, as he'd already seen her in bathers, but disrobing in front of someone implied intimacy. Besides, she'd taken another step down the confidence road today and worn the new bikini she'd bought in Noumea, and if the way he'd been staring at her over lunch was any indication, she'd be blushing from head to foot the entire time.

She dropped her bag on the sand and whipped her dress over her head, kicked off her sandals and rummaged in her bag for sunscreen. Just as she started to rub the lotion on her arm, he touched her hand.

'I can do that for you.'

She squeezed the tube so tight lotion spurted out in a noisy raspberry. 'I'm fine. You go ahead. I'll meet you out there shortly.'

He didn't budge, and held out his hand for the tube. 'Unless you're a contortionist I doubt you'll be able to reach your back. This sun can burn you in less than ten seconds flat, so let me help.'

He was right, but the thought of him rubbing any part of her body was already causing the skin behind her ears to prickle in that annoying way only he and strawberries could elicit.

'Really, I'm fine—'

'Damn, you're a stubborn woman.'

He snatched the lotion out of her hand and squeezed a healthy blob into his palm, raising an eyebrow when she frowned. 'Now why don't you play nice and lie face-down on your towel?'

With an exaggerated huff, she plopped on the towel, rested her forehead on her hands and braced herself for the first cold dollop of lotion.

'I suppose you want me to thank you?'

'Oh, you will.'

He thoughtfully warmed the lotion between his hands, though his first touch was as shocking, as electrifying, as if he'd squeezed the entire tube onto her back.

She gritted her teeth and tried to relax under his hands, while her skin tingled everywhere he touched.

She'd never been touched by a man like this before. Jax hadn't been touchy-feely, and his version of foreplay extended to a kiss and wandering hands.

She'd never experienced the luxury of a man's warm, firm touch gliding over her skin, and as platonic as this was, she couldn't help but enjoy it.

'You're very tense.'

'Must be the extra aerobic classes.' *As if.*

He didn't let up the pressure, his hands stroking her back in long sweeps designed to be impersonal yet driving her just a little bit mad with the sheer pleasure of it.

'Try to relax.'

How could she relax when he was stroking her flesh, his strong hands splaying over her back, her defences unravelling as fast as her muscles unwound?

His fingers kept snagging the tie of her bikini bra, though she didn't dare suggest he undo it. That would be *her* final undoing. She might be immune to his charms, but her body, long neglected, was enjoying this way too much.

'Why don't you turn over, and I'll do your front too?'

Just like that, her muscles twanged back to tense. The thought of him rubbing her stomach sent heat surging to her cheeks.

'Not a good idea.'

She flipped onto her back and held out her hand for the tube.

'Why not?'

'Because I'm perfectly capable of rubbing lotion onto my tummy.'

His eyes glittered and she shivered at their taunting glint. 'But where's the fun in that?'

Her skin prickled some more and she itched behind her ear.

'Give me the tube.'

He held it overhead and waved it around. 'Only if you ask nicely.'

Clenching her jaw, she stuck her hand under his nose. 'Please.'

He chuckled, and dropped the tube into her palm. 'Actually, it'll probably be just as much fun watching you do it.'

'Pervert.'

'Just interested. But you already know that.'

His low, suggestive tone had her squeezing way too much lotion into her palm, and rather than taking her time to ensure she didn't miss any spots she slapped the stuff onto her belly and made a few half-hearted circles before leaping from the sand.

'Right. Hope that water's warm.'

'It's perfect.'

His heated gaze slid over her before meeting hers and she bit the inside of her lip to stop it quivering. He totally unnerved her, from his roguish smile to the devilish glint in his eyes.

He was toying with her, she knew it, but with every compliment she let her guard down just that little bit more.

She wanted to believe him, wanted to believe he thought she was perfect. But she wasn't a fool. Not anymore. Objectively, how could he find her less-than-a-handful breasts—another Jax-ism she hated—no waist to speak of, and thighs with the first hint of dimples perfect?

'Oh-oh, you've got that serious look on your face. Come on—race you there!'

He flung the words over his shoulder and took off, tearing across the hot sand before she could move. By the time she'd caught up he'd dived into the water.

'Not fair. You've got longer legs.'

'Nothing wrong with your legs, from what I can see.'

Rolling her eyes, she waded into the cerulean lagoon, sighing at the blissful feel of the water.

'Now, if you hold off on the flirting for just a few minutes, I might actually enjoy this swim.'

He pushed her head under water in response.

She spluttered and spat salt water as she surfaced, clawing at him, trying to return the favour, only to have him slip out of her grip.

'You're in trouble, sailor boy.'

They tumbled in the water for the next few minutes, arms and legs flailing wildly, laughing so hard she got a cramp.

She couldn't remember the last time she'd had this much fun. Her long work hours weren't conducive to play, and when she went to the beach at the weekend it was to swim for exercise rather than leisure.

When they finally emerged, she clutched her side. 'You've given me a stitch.'

'Good. I've never seen you laugh like that.'

He touched her cheek, a brief, fleeting glance that had her fingers digging painfully into her side to stop herself reaching up and touching the skin he just had.

'That's because you're not that funny.'

'Ouch.'

He laid both hands over his heart and she chuckled.

'The day I wound that enormous ego of yours is the day I'll go skinny-dipping in the Pacific Ocean.'

'I'm wounded! I'm wounded!'

He fell to the sand in a pathetic heap, writhing as if he'd just been stung by a lethal jellyfish, and she laughed.

'I'm going to dry off. When you've finished with the theatrics, I'll see you up there.'

She pointed to the palm trees and headed off, ignoring his call of, 'You're no fun.'

She knew he'd meant it as a joke, a fly-away comment, but the words echoed as she towelled off.

She wasn't fun—didn't know how to have fun. Not when she'd spent her whole life trying to do the right thing.

Beth had once called her a nerd, and she'd shrugged, pushed her tortoiseshell glasses up her nose and scuffed her sensible shoes, agreeing with the assessment but hurt all the same.

Everyone saw her the same way: no fun. People at work, her cousin, even Zac—and while his opinion shouldn't matter, considering she wouldn't see him after the end of next week, it did. As he joined her, and she watched water droplets run in rivulets down his muscular torso as he bent to pick up his towel, she really, really wished her newfound confidence extended to having a little fun.

'I'm just going to dry off in the sun for a while,' she said. And blink away the sudden sting of tears for feeling inadequate and inexperienced and inept.

'Don't be too long. These UVs can seriously burn.'

She grabbed her towel and laid it on the sand a few feet away—an ill-chosen spot, considering she had a clear view of him stretched flat on his back—his long, lean body, his abdominals composed of ridges of hard muscle…

She squeezed her eyes shut to blot out the tempting

image, and must have dozed, for it seemed like an eternity later when his voice roused her.

'Excuse me, sun goddess, you should come into the shade now.'

Her eyes fluttered open and she stretched, feeling rested and composed and completely tear-free.

'Nice of you to be so concerned.'

She picked up her towel and flung it next to his, putting enough space between them to ensure no accidental contact.

'I'll admit my concern is altruistic. I don't want to rub lotion on you again.'

'Why's that?'

'I enjoyed it way too much.'

His gaze trailed over her body, lingering on every area he'd rubbed earlier and everywhere in between, and darn it if that prickly itch didn't start up again.

She quirked an eyebrow. 'If you enjoyed something as mundane as rubbing suntan lotion on my back, you must get out even less than I do.'

He leaned forward, too close, too masculine—too everything. 'Go on—admit it.'

She bit her lip, inched back. 'Admit what?'

'You enjoyed it too.'

His grin was pure temptation, and she waved her hand in front of her face as if swatting away a particularly bothersome fly.

'The only thing I'll admit is finding your incessant flirting extremely tiresome.'

His smile faded at the same moment the sun ducked behind a cloud. Both left her slightly chilled.

'Do you really feel that way?' he asked.

Her heart stuttered as she searched for a suitable answer. What could she say? That she didn't believe his compliments? That her self-confidence was so shot by a guy who'd used slick words before that she couldn't trust easily? That she wished she could believe one tenth of his attention was real and not just his natural instinct to charm? That she hid behind sharp retorts, using them as a barrier against her insecurities?

She settled for semi-truth, feeling a tad guilty her barb had tarnished what had been an enjoyable day.

'Honestly? I'm not used to the attention.'

He couldn't have looked more surprised if she'd stripped off in front of him.

'You said things ended with your ex three years ago, but you date, right?'

Heck, look what she'd got herself into now. She could lie, but she'd always been lousy at it. Beth said her mouth had pursed into a strange prune shape the few times she'd tried it, and she already had him staring at her as if she was nuts.

'My last date was with George Clooney, Brad Pitt and Matt Damon.'

He smiled. '*Ocean's Eleven* fan, huh?'

'Oh, yeah.'

He reached out, touched her hand. She flinched, silently cursing her reaction.

'Hell, Lana, I'm not some kind of monster. I like you. I want to get to know you better.'

She shook her head, using her hair as a shield to hide her face. 'What's the point? I'm off the ship next week, so why get to know each other?'

'Because it could be fun.'

Her gaze snapped to his. She was surprised by the serious glint in those deep blue eyes. She'd seen him cheeky, teasing, even wicked, but it was the first time she'd seen this solemn expression fixing her with concern.

'Fun? The only fun a guy like you would be interested in over the next week is a fling. And I'm not that kind of girl.'

His eyes darkened to midnight, disappointment flickering in their depths. 'You don't have a very high opinion of me, do you?'

She shrugged, hating that they were having this conversation, hating that she'd put a dampener on what had been a lovely day.

'You're a guy. You're a sailor. You meet women all the time. You're a master at flirting. The only reason you're paying me any attention is because of that stupid challenge I threw down the first night on the spur of the moment, because I couldn't think of anything else quick enough to get rid of you.' She took a deep breath, a steadying breath, clenching her hands to stop them from shaking. 'It's nothing personal. I understand that. You see me as some sort of challenge because I'm not falling at your feet like the rest of the female population probably does. You—'

'You're wrong. Dead wrong.'

He leaped from his towel and started pacing the sand with long, angry strides that showed he was wrestling with something. The truth, perhaps?

'Am I?'

Her almost-whisper stopped him dead and he swivelled to face her, dropping down on his knees in front of her.

'Damn straight. Want to know why you're here with me today, on my one day off a week?'

She waved her hand. 'Go ahead. I'm sure you'll tell me anyway.'

His hands shot out, cradling her face in their warm, firm grip before she could blink.

'Because I like you. *You*. Not your clothes, or your willingness to help me out, or because I want you to sleep with me. You. You're funny and smart and you make me laugh.'

'So now I'm a clown—'

'Shut up.'

He kissed her—a soft, tender kiss that reached down to her soul, shattering her defences along the way, scaring her beyond belief.

'Now, it's time to head back. And I don't want to hear another word.' She opened her mouth and he pressed his finger to it. 'Not one word. Not another character assassination. Not another assumption. Not one word unless you agree to play nice. Got it?'

Her lips twitched, and his answering smile made her heart sing.

He wasn't asking for anything, didn't expect her to sleep with him, and hadn't belittled her when he'd heard the sorry truth about her inexperience with men.

So what should she do? Spend some more time with him? Get to know him better? With the aim to do what?

He had his life on the sea. She had a great apartment in Sydney, a few colleagues she could call friends at a pinch, and a good job at the museum. They didn't have a future, no matter how well they got to know each other.

'Come on. Stop thinking so much.'

He held out his hand, and for the second time in as many hours she silenced her voice of reason and took hold of it.

'How about we go with the flow, see what happens over the next week? How much trouble can we get into in seven days?'

She raised an eyebrow, and he grinned as a scary thought flitted through her mind.

Plenty.

CHAPTER NINE

THOUGH she would have preferred silence, they made desultory small talk on the drive back to the ship, as a multitude of thoughts swirled through her mind—most of them focussed on the man sitting next to her.

She'd never met anyone like him.

Confident and charming, yet astute enough to look beyond the surface and home in on exactly what she wanted: a guy to recognise she had a brain, a sense of humour, and a yearning not to be taken for granted.

She couldn't believe he'd said all that stuff, had seriously cracked the protective shield around her heart with his sincerity.

So what now? She wouldn't have the guts for a fling, no matter how far her confidence soared. She couldn't do something like that unless she was emotionally involved. And while Zac said he liked her, *like* didn't equate to what she craved: a lifelong love from an incredible man who'd put her first.

Completely moronic, completely delusional, completely crazy, but she'd been dreaming of her own happily-ever-after for so long she'd somehow taken his genuine niceness and tangled him up in her fantasy.

She cast a sideways glance at his profile and sighed, her heart hoping for a minor miracle while her head shouted, *Wake up and smell the sea air.*

'What are you thinking?'

'Not much.' He really, really didn't want to know.

'I can hear your mind ticking from here.'

'If you're that perceptive, you tell me.'

'I think you're mulling over what I said back at the cove. Close?'

There he went again, being way too perceptive.

'Don't give up your day job. You'd make a lousy mind-reader.'

'So?'

'So you told me not to say anything unless it was nice, and I'm having a hard time coming up with anything.'

His chuckles warmed her better than the sun's rays. 'See—that's why I like you. Every prickly, cynical, blunt inch of you.'

'Yeah, well, I can't help it if you've been spending too long in this tropical heat.'

He slowed the Jeep and turned onto the dock. 'You know, you can hide behind that smart mouth of yours all you like, but I'm going to get to know you better whether you like it or not.'

'Yeah?'

He stopped the engine and turned to her, his slow, sexy smile sending a shiver through her. 'Yeah. Don't say I didn't warn you.'

Charming sailor boy she could handle. Single-minded sailor boy with a determined glint in his too-blue eyes had her plans to hold him off sinking faster than the *Titanic*.

Hoping her voice didn't quiver, she aimed for flippant. 'I stand duly warned. Thanks for the tour.'

'My pleasure. Hope it lived up to your expectations.'

If she'd had any he'd blown them clean out of the water with his shrewd observations back at the cove. She didn't want to get involved with a guy like him. But what if it was too late?

'Uh-huh.'

'Great. I better get this Jeep back to Raj. See you at dinner?'

She nodded, the thought of spending more time with him after the day they'd just had sending a tiny helix of joy interwoven with doubt spiralling through her.

He winked, sent her a jaunty half-salute, and drove away, leaving her mind spinning and her tummy tossing with nerves at the many possible ways he could 'get to know her' over the next few days.

Zac pulled up at the front of Raj's and switched off the engine, wishing he could switch off his thoughts as easily.

Things were out of control. Or, more to the point, things with Lana were out of control.

After lunch and his chat with Sujit he'd been all gung-ho, determined to explore the possibility of a relationship with her. Then they'd talked at the cove and things had rushed downhill from there.

He'd known she was inexperienced—but not even dating? Hell, did that mean she was a virgin too? No way. She'd had that moronic ex—not that that meant much—and there was the way she'd responded to his kisses, the way she had that funny gleam in her eyes at times. But what did that mean? That she had a bit of sass lurking beneath her prudish front?

He didn't dally with virgins. In fact he didn't dally with women, period, considering it took all his concentration these days to perpetrate his plan.

But he wasn't fooling around with Lana. Had known that the instant she'd made her true opinion of him clear.

He'd kissed her to shut her up, to demonstrate what she really meant to him—a gentle, soft kiss, when he'd been hankering to devour her all day.

He wasn't toying with her. He wasn't just after a fling. So what could he do to prove it to her?

He got out of the car and headed for the house. Considering Raj's happy marriage and five kids, maybe he could give him a pointer or two.

As he reached the veranda of the whitewashed bungalow, Raj stepped out. 'Hello, my friend. Had a good day?'

'Yeah. Thanks for the Jeep. I had a great time down at the cove.'

'I'm sure you did. Sujit phoned me and said you had a beautiful lady companion with you today.'

He groaned. 'I can't believe you two old gossips.'

Raj's grin broadened. 'He also said you were so ga-ga over this woman you could hardly finish your dahl. Must be serious. Care to tell me more?'

'Maybe. Though I'd kill for a cold beer first.'

Raj clapped both hands to his head. 'Where are my manners? Come in.'

As Zac sank into a comfortable cane chair with a beer in his hand, Raj raised an eyebrow.

'So my friend. Time to tell all.'

He had two choices: stay silent and listen to the hum of the ceiling fan, or get an objective perspective on a situation that was complicated at best.

'Lana's different from anyone I've ever met. I want to get to know her better, but I only have a week before I head to Europe. Not enough time to really get involved.'

Especially when the likelihood of her retreating back

into her shell was high. He'd seen her growing confidence—the perfume, staying on after the kiss last night, the hot new bikini today—but small changes didn't mean she wouldn't retreat at the first sign of an over-eager sailor laying a possible future relationship on her after knowing her for a week.

He took a long slug of beer, savouring the icy brew sliding down his throat. 'That's the short version.'

'Do you have to return to Europe?'

He nodded. He'd let his uncle down once before. Not this time. He'd make sure of it.

'Jimmy's sick again. The cancer's back and it's spread.'

Raj's bleak expression mirrored his. 'I'm sorry. Is it—?'

'Terminal? Yeah.' He downed most of his beer in one gulp, hating the injustice of this disease that had no cure and robbed a man of his health, his dignity, his life.

'How much time?'

He shrugged. 'He's seen all the best docs in London and had varying opinions. Some say six months; some say a year, max.'

Raj shook his head and clicked his tongue. 'Very sad.'

'He says he wants to be left alone, but I know the stubborn old coot better than I know myself. That's why I'm moving head office to London for the next year. So I can visit him whether he damn well likes it or not.'

'Ah…' Raj nodded like a wise old guru. 'So this is the problem with your woman. She lives in Australia and you'll be based in London for at least the next twelve months?'

Zac leaned forward, rested his head in his hands. 'It's more complex than that.'

'Matters of the heart often are.'

He leaped out of his chair and started pacing, wishing

he hadn't mentioned Lana to his friend. 'Why are we even having this conversation?'

'Because you have fallen, and fallen hard.'

He pulled up short. 'You know the biggest problem? I've lied to her, and she's a straightforward, no-nonsense person. She's been lied to before and it cut her up badly. How the hell am I going to tell her the truth now, when she barely trusts me as it is?'

Raj's eyebrows shot heavenward. 'She doesn't know your true profession?'

'No. You know secrecy's been paramount, to give me a chance to catch our saboteur. And I only met her a week ago.'

'For a woman you only met a week ago, you're sure doing a lot of soul-searching.'

Zac picked up his beer and slugged the rest, desperate to ease the dryness in his throat. 'Crazy, isn't it? Happily single for years, then I take one look at this quirky, captivating woman and can't get her out of my mind.'

'If she cares for you, she'll forgive you. Besides, it's only a little white lie. You have worked on ships as a public relations manager. You just also happen to manage the entire fleet.' Raj chuckled, doing little to soothe Zac's nerves.

'I'm glad you find this situation amusing.'

'You're really in a bind, aren't you?'

'I feel so much better after talking with you.'

'Sarcasm won't help, my friend. I suggest you go back to your ship and think long and hard about your dilemma of the heart.'

'Very poetic,' Zac muttered, knowing all the soul-searching in the world wouldn't get him out of this quandary. The way he saw it, there was only one solution: tell her the truth, start a relationship with her now and pray she'd be interested in continuing it.

Though he'd never been a fan of long-distance relationships, had seen them consistently fall apart around him over the many years he'd worked on ships, the thought of keeping in touch with her till he returned to Sydney, maybe seeing her on the odd flying visit, sent a thrill of hope through him.

'You know, between you and Sujit you two old reprobates could start your own relationship counselling service.'

Raj laughed, picked up the car keys and slapped him on the back. 'Come on, I'll drop you off. Everything will work out for the best.'

He grunted in response and hoped to God his friend was right.

Lana finished her aerobics class still feeling stressed, despite rave reviews from the participants. How could she keep her mind on the job when flashes of her afternoon with Zac kept popping into her mind at the most inopportune moments?

Take the rowing machine: it reminded her of boats, which reminded her of water, which reminded her of beaches and ultimately Zac.

The treadmill wasn't much better: walking hand in hand to the pristine lagoon, with Zac.

As for her towel, slung casually over a set of free weights, she wouldn't even go there, considering her skin prickled at the mere thought of his hands stroking her back while she'd been lying on that towel.

Thankfully, she made it back to her cabin without any more flashbacks, though once she set foot in the small space and closed the door she slumped against it.

Of all the fish in the sea, she had to get hooked by a sailor.

She smiled at the pun, though there was nothing funny

about the situation. She was falling for him. There was only so much a girl could take, and with that non-stop charm chipping away at her defences almost twenty-four-seven what hope did she have?

Considering he was a sailor and she was merely a land-lubber, they had little hope of making a relationship work. Especially the type of relationship she wanted: husband, kids, noisy Sunday afternoons in her very own backyard, rolling in autumn leaves with her brood, face-painting, playing tag, scoffing sticky toffee apples. The kind of childhood she'd never had. The kind of childhood she'd yearned for.

Beth understood. She'd wanted the same thing: they'd role-played happy families countless times as lonely six-year-olds, when their mums had died in the same car crash.

Beth had found her happily-ever-after, and while Lana was pleased for her cousin there wasn't a day that passed when she didn't secretly crave the same for herself.

Taking this cruise had been a first. Well, chalk up another—it was also the first time she'd met a guy who saw beneath her prissy veneer; the first time since Jax that she'd trusted a guy enough to get to know him better; the first time she'd felt real passion, if his kisses were anything to go by, and she knew without a doubt that if the last of her defences totally crumbled it would be the first time she'd fallen in love.

A knock on the door made her jump, and she opened it to find the man intruding on her thoughts filling the doorway, looking incredible as usual in full uniform, the gold embroidery on his epaulettes catching the light.

'Hey, there.'

'Hi.'

Why was it that every time he caught her unawares

her ability to respond coherently vanished as fast as her resistance?

She dropped her gaze, taking in his polished dress shoes, his long legs in formal black trousers and the white jacket ending just below his waist. She usually laughed at men wearing monkey jackets, yet on Zac it accentuated his butt.

'How did the class go?'

'Great.'

If she discounted her obsessing over inanimate fitness equipment and how it reminded her of him.

'Just wanted to let you know I won't make dinner tonight. Business calls, but maybe we can catch up later? The ship sails at ten, and it's a magical sight as we pull away from dock, so how about we meet under the bridge then?'

She hesitated. Was this wise? Spending more time with him when he'd said he wanted to get to know her better despite her resistance? Giving him the opportunity to chip away at her emotional barriers even more, to the point where they might disintegrate once and for all?

Maybe it was the wariness he glimpsed in her eyes, maybe the hint of uncertainty tugging at her mouth, but he stepped forward and touched her hand.

'Come on, you know you'll miss me at dinner. This way I'm just trying to make up for lost time.'

She laughed, as he'd intended, his charismatic smile disarming her quicker than she could say land ahoy.

'Okay. I need to sharpen up a few barbs.'

He squeezed her hand before releasing it. 'Great. I'll see you there just before ten.'

For the second time in as many minutes she leaned against the closed door, her head filled with Zac, her heart filled with foreboding.

* * *

'Hello, sailor.'

Zac straightened from where he'd been leaning on a railing, a poster boy for the gorgeous nautical male, silhouetted against the bridge, an appreciative gleam in his eyes. A misplaced gleam, considering she wore a boring black calf-length skirt and an olive top which had seen better days.

'Glad you made it.'

'Didn't think I would, huh?'

'I had my doubts, considering it's probably past your bedtime.'

She chuckled and waved a finger back and forth in front of him. 'Hey, I'm supposed to be the one practising barbs, not you.'

'Maybe we can practise together?'

His voice dropped lower and he wiggled his eyebrows suggestively. She shook her head, unable to keep a smile off her face.

'You're hopeless.'

'Your fault.' He sniffed the air like a hound, coming closer, too close, almost nuzzling her neck. 'You're wearing that damn perfume again. Any wonder I'm a broken man? Didn't I warn you that stuff was dangerous?'

'It's the only perfume I own.'

Maybe she could blame the perfume for her gradual melting towards him? Ever since she'd worn it her resistance had slowly but surely unravelled.

His low, sexy chuckle had her clutching the rail for support, all too aware that her collapsing resolve had little to do with the fragrance and more to do with the man staring at her with desire in his eyes.

'Well, if you keep wearing it you're definitely heading for a whole lot of trouble.'

Heat flushed her cheeks and she gripped the rail so hard her knuckles stood out. 'Oooh, I'm scared.'

'You should be.'

And for one crazy, loaded second as he leaned towards her she almost welcomed the danger of having a guy like him interested in her.

Clearing her throat, she deliberately relaxed her fingers and straightened. 'So, where's this magical sight you promised me?'

'Be careful what you wish for.'

His deep voice rippled over her like a silken caress, and her knees almost buckled right then and there.

As if on cue, the ship's horn blasted as the massive vessel pulled away from the dock. Suva's lights twinkled like a fairyland as the ship sailed up the channel, and a gentle breeze fanned her face—a welcome relief for her fiery cheeks.

She was no good at this. Even with him being so nice this afternoon, even with her defences lowered, she still couldn't throw herself into flirting unreservedly.

Hiding away was a habit of a lifetime. She'd done it as a child, leaving her dad to work through his grief, and she'd done it as a teenager, flying under the radar of her father's countless girlfriends who had waltzed in and out of a revolving door.

No prizes for guessing where her abhorrence of casual sex came from. Her folks had had the perfect relationship, with their love for each other radiating out to include her. They'd been the epitome of the happy family before that car accident had ripped their lives apart.

Her dad had always assured her she'd come first in his life and she had. He'd mourned her mum for seven long years before dating again. But she had never understood the women who could jump into bed so quickly when her dad made it perfectly clear he wasn't interested in a relationship—never understood what motivated them to be so free and easy with something she considered a gift.

'Well, what do you think?'

Her gaze swept the horizon, the sea. Eventually she raised her eyes to meet his, which were firmly fixed on her rather than the view. 'You're right. It's magical.'

His eyes glittered in the moonlight, a sexy smile curved his lips, and the skin behind her ears gave an alarming prickle.

'You're not looking at the view,' she said.

'I prefer this one.'

She tensed as he lowered his head, barely grazing her lips, and the feather-light kiss sabotaged her initial determination to pull away, rendering her resolve to keep her distance useless.

He kissed her again and again and again, gently increasing the pressure with each kiss as a languorous heat stole from her lips to her fingertips—a heat she'd never experienced, a heat that stole through her body and into her heart.

He hadn't laid a hand on her, yet every inch of her skin tingled as if he'd caressed it, and their lack of contact only served to increase the pleasure of their lips locked together, tasting, sampling, searching in an endless quest for satisfaction.

But she couldn't give him satisfaction—at least not the kind a virile man like him wanted, deserved. She pulled away, wishing she was another type of woman, wishing she had the courage to let go of her reservations all at once, throw caution to the wind and see what happened.

'Definitely magical.' He touched her lips, still quivering from the impact of his kisses, with a reverent fingertip, gently tracing the contours, undoing her one little stroke at a time.

She needed to reassemble her wits, to say something, but her mind wouldn't co-operate while her body was still in shock.

'I take it this is part of your plan to get to know me better?'

As if she'd tripped a silent trigger, the shutters descended over his eyes and his smile faded. 'Plan?'

She shrugged and wrapped her arms around her middle, suddenly chilled despite the balmy breeze. She had to say this—had to be bluntly honest. It was the only way she knew. 'You're trying to seduce me.'

'Am I?'

His sombre expression, the way his voice tightened, the distance he'd established between them by taking a step back, all indicated one thing: she'd insulted him.

Tugging on the end of her ponytail, matted by the wind, she met his bitter gaze head-on.

'Come on—level with me. I may be some naïve recluse who hasn't been on a date in far too long, but I'm not stupid. You said you like me. A guy like you has needs. So what I want to know is this. Why are you going through this game of charming me, kissing me, when there isn't a hope in hell I'll sleep with you?'

There—she'd said it. And while her gut churned with trepidation, her hands were surprisingly steady as she folded them in front of her, before realising she probably looked like a prim and proper nun and promptly released them.

A vein pulsed at his temple as he raked a hand through his hair, dishevelled and spiked and thoroughly tempting. Then he met her gaze, his clouded with disappointment, hers wary yet relieved that she'd asked what had been bugging her since that afternoon.

She'd had the guts to speak her mind, and he had no idea what a big deal that was.

'This isn't just about sex.'

'Oh, really?'

He jammed his hands in his pockets, shoulders squared, back rigid. 'I meant what I said this afternoon. I want to spend time with you, get to know you. But I'll be damned if I stand here and lie about wanting to drag you back to my cabin right this very minute and have amazing sex with you all night long.'

Her mouth dropped open, a squeaky 'oh' escaping before she shut it.

His eyes flashed blue fire as he fixed her with a steely gaze. 'There. Is that what you wanted to hear? Do I want to have sex with you? Hell, yeah. But I'm not going to push you. If you want me half as much as I want you, you'll have to show me.'

She bit her tongue, biding her time, trying to unscramble her brain long enough to answer, to give him a response halfway decipherable that didn't consist of another scintillating 'oh'.

Her hands trembled and her belly rolled in time with the ship as it headed out to the open sea. She searched for the words to make him understand half of what she was feeling: confused, scared, excited, a mish-mash of emotions that terrified her as much as falling for this incredible man who pulled no punches and spoke the truth without flinching.

Honesty was all-important to her—one of her top criteria in her perfect man, courtesy of the elaborate lies Jax had told to manipulate her. She'd never trust a liar again, and here was a guy who was dead-set honest about what he wanted. She admired him for it, even though the blunt truth of exactly what he wanted from her scared her beyond belief.

After a drawn-out silence, he reached out and she let him take her hand.

'Look, I'm sorry for laying all that on you. But you have to know you're driving me crazy.'

'Totally unintentional, I can assure you.'

His mouth kicked up at her wry answer and hers twitched in response.

'Do you want me to back off? Slow down? Just say the word.'

Oh-oh. It was like being given a choice between a decadent double choc fudge sundae—something wickedly indulgent she knew she'd end up regretting later—and a single scoop of vanilla—plain, boring. She knew exactly what she'd get if she took the safe option.

Did she want him to back off? Really?

Her head said it was the logical thing to do, considering she'd be off the ship shortly, but her heart was giving strange little twangs it never had before, quietly urging her to take a risk for once in her sedate life.

Maybe it was her turn for a dose of healthy reality? If he ran, it wasn't meant to be. If he didn't… Well, she'd face that frightening prospect if it arose.

Taking a deep breath, she went for broke. 'I can't get physical with a guy unless I'm emotionally involved. That's just me. And I hate to break it to you, but I wouldn't have let you kiss me just now unless I wasn't already starting to invest some emotion in us.'

Understanding, stark and pure, splintered in his eyes before coalescing into a bright, hard blue.

'I've kissed you before.'

She waved away his comment. 'Impulse kisses. You turning on the charm.'

'And tonight?'

After the time they'd spent together, after she'd grown to trust him through his actions—he hadn't pushed her for sex once, despite his admission just now of how much he wanted it—emotion had more than clouded her judgment. It had taken over to the point she didn't know why she was holding him at bay any more.

She raised her eyes to his, silently imploring him to understand. 'Tonight I've realised you've crept under my guard. And I'm starting to like it.'

The first flicker of awareness in his steady gaze made her want to execute a perfect swan dive into the ocean.

'How much?'

Drawing on her meagre reserve of resolve, she placed a tentative hand on his chest. 'A lot.'

He caressed her cheek softly, lingering for an exquisite moment. 'Then where do we go from here?'

Damned if she knew.

After Zac had walked Lana back to her cabin, he headed for the place he did his best thinking: the bridge.

Ever since he'd joined the fleet as a young, eager sailor he'd loved this control centre of a ship, the hub that drove these monstrous vessels. He loved the quiet efficiency of the staff going about their business, he loved the view, and—like any guy—he loved the gadgets. Hundreds of them, that beeped and lit up and made his fingers itch to touch them.

He usually popped up here on the pretext of consulting with the Captain over something, when in reality he loved the buzz, the feeling of control. He now owned this baby, and the decisions he made could drive her and the rest of the fleet further than the company had ever been before.

Ironic, considering he had no control over his situation

with Lana. Or, more precisely, control over his burgeoning feelings.

He couldn't believe what she'd just told him. Sure, he'd caught the odd gleam in her eyes that said she was thawing towards him in the attraction stakes—not to mention her genuine responses to his kisses—but to say she was emotionally involved?

Hell. It blew him away.

It was exactly what he wanted—what he'd hoped for to lead into a full-blown long-distance relationship, whatever that might entail.

The kicker was she'd given him the perfect opportunity to say he was emotionally involved too, but he'd held back.

For, no matter how long he stewed over this, hashing out scenarios, it all came back to Uncle Jimmy and the fact he couldn't let him down—couldn't let the man who'd given him everything die alone.

Which meant he'd be on the other side of the world for a year, a whole three hundred and sixty-five days, and he'd be damned if he expected her to wait for him for that length of time. She deserved more.

Besides, he'd travelled down this road before, with Magda waiting at home for him, and it had killed his marriage. She'd changed while he'd been away, irrevocably, and there'd been no going back.

But Lana wasn't Magda, and he owed it to her—to himself—to let her make the decision.

Rubbing a hand across the back of his neck, he sank into the nearest chair, leaned back and focussed on the control panel in front of him.

He had to give her the option—had to know he'd tried his damnedest to make it work with this quick-witted, infuriatingly shy, naturally beautiful woman. She was worth it—every unaffected inch of her.

He just hoped she cared enough to take the risk.

CHAPTER TEN

FEELING like a pawn in a romantic game of her own making, the last thing Lana wanted to do several mornings later was play chess, but she had a game scheduled with Mavis and she hated to let her down.

She plopped into a comfy armchair and ordered a double espresso from a waiter, hoping the after-affects of yet another sleepless night didn't show. She'd had to use concealer to hide the dark rings under her eyes for the first time ever. Beth would be proud she even knew what the stuff was for.

'Guess what arrived at my door this morning?'

Lana screwed her eyes tight, pretending to think. 'Let me guess. One of those dance hosts you're so fond of?'

Mavis roared with laughter. 'Bad girl. Next best thing, though: an invitation to the Captain's cocktail party tonight. I'm sure there'll be a few eligible men there to bat my eye-lashes at.'

'You're supposed to be setting me a good example.'

'Hah!' Mavis snorted. 'I think it's too late for you, my girl. You don't need any lessons, if that happy glow is any indication. I take it your tour went well the other day?'

The tour? It seemed like a lifetime ago, considering what had happened since. The chat they'd had the night the ship had left Suva had been replayed at will, over and over, till she wondered if she was going crazy. Luckily Zac had been tied up with work since, and she'd barely seen him. Maybe telling him she felt emotionally involved with him had been a good thing? Perhaps it had driven him away once and for all?

Indecision tore at her. She wanted to tell her friend everything, but was still trying to understand it herself, so she gave her a brief version of events instead. Mavis nodded in all the right spots, waiting till she'd finished.

'Have you fallen in love?'

Lana sighed, resigned to the truth. 'He's a sailor, married to his job. What hope have I got?'

'Have you told him how you feel?'

'Sort of.'

She'd told him she had feelings—of a kind. Invested emotion meant the same thing, right?

But they hadn't resolved anything that night. After she'd dropped her little 'emotion' bombshell they'd talked around it, he'd made one of his charming comments, she'd fired back a quick retort, and he'd walked her back to her cabin—*sans* kiss.

Besides, nothing would happen unless she wanted it to. He'd made that pretty darn clear.

'What does "sort of" mean?' Mavis touched a pawn, moved it forward by keeping her finger on it, frowned in concentration before moving it back. 'Some newfangled term you young people have for chickening out?'

Lana chuckled. 'Yeah, something like that.'

Mavis glanced up and fixed her with a stern glare. 'So what are you going to do, missy? You need to show him how you feel. Take a risk. See what happens.'

She had to *show* him. He'd said the same thing.

Would she have the courage to make a play for the man she'd fallen for?

As she watched Mavis toy with the pawn again, a glimmer of an idea shimmered through her consciousness, slowly coalescing into a plan that had her tummy clenching with nerves.

Did she have the gumption to pull it off?

'Listen to your heart, dear. It's the only way.'

Listening to her heart was what had got her to this point: confused, elated, petrified, yet buzzing with anticipation. Ironic, as she'd always listened to her head until now, had been the perfect curator, the perfect cousin, the perfect girlfriend.

She had a well-ordered, perfectly sensible life back in Sydney. So why was she looking to turn it topsy-turvy by getting involved with a guy like Zac?

She gestured at the chessboard. 'Your move. Then I might tell you my plan.'

'What plan?' Mavis's eyes gleamed with delight at the hint of subterfuge.

Lana chuckled. 'What time do you think you'll be ready tonight?'

'Well, there's a lot more of me to nip, tuck, polish, exfoliate, moisturise and pluck than you, so around six?'

Lana smiled and moved a bishop. 'That's fine. If you could meet me at my cabin shortly after, that'd be great.'

Mavis frowned. 'But what's the plan?'

She leaned forward and crooked her finger, dropping her voice to a conspiratorial whisper. 'I need your help.'

'How about this one?'

Lana glanced at the skimpy, thigh-skimming crimson silk dress and shook her head. 'I couldn't wear that.'

Mavis shrugged, flung it on the ever-growing pile on her bed, and picked another dress off a hanger from the quickly emptying wardrobe. 'What about this?'

Lana took one look at the skin-tight tangerine tube dress and wrinkled her nose. 'No way.'

Mavis sighed and added it to the pile. 'This cousin of yours sure has an interesting dress sense.'

'Way out, more like it.'

Beth had packed enough designer dresses to last Lana a month, but every one she'd contemplated wearing tonight had ended up on the discard pile. And, considering she'd have to make a decision shortly or do a Lady Godiva, her chances of finding anything suitable were rapidly dwindling.

'This one?' Mavis held a mulberry mini at arm's length, screwing up her eyes with a thoughtful look on her face. 'The colour's gorgeous.'

As was the dress. The fabric shimmered like the finest claret as Mavis turned it this way and that. But the dress was super-short, redefining the term 'mini', and she'd never be able to pull off something like that without tugging self-consciously at the hem all night.

She wanted to make a statement, to show Zac what she wanted—not show him what *he* apparently wanted!

'Here, let me hold it up to you.'

The second Mavis held it up in front of her and she glanced down and saw where the dress ended she shook her head vigorously. 'Next.'

Mavis tut-tutted as she reached into the wardrobe again. 'There are only a few left.'

Her heart sank. She'd seen what was left. She'd examined every single dress in there at least ten times since she'd made her decision this morning to go all out tonight and prove to Zac she was ready to take the next step.

She always came back to the same dress: a stunning floor-length formal gown in the richest shot-silk jade, its strapless bodice embroidered with tiny emerald crystals designed to capture the light and draw attention to the bust.

The gown was a stand-out—the type of dress to make a statement, the type of dress fit for a princess, the type of dress to turn an ugly duckling like her into a rare swan.

But she'd balked at trying it on, a small part of her terrified she wouldn't live up to a dress like that no matter how far she'd come in the confidence stakes.

She heard Mavis flicking hangers at a rapid pace, and knew the exact moment she caught sight of *the* dress.

'Oh, my.'

Mavis clasped her heart, drew out the jade sheath with reverence. 'I swear, if you say no to this one I'm marching out of this cabin right now.'

Lana gnawed on her bottom lip, twisted one of the few curls left hanging from the elaborate do Mavis had managed with a few bobby pins and a squirt of hairspray.

'Well?'

'I like it, but—'

'No buts. This is the one.' Mavis held it up to her and sighed. 'Perfect. You should see what this colour does to your eyes. That young man of yours won't know what's hit him when he sees you in this.'

That was all that mattered, really. What Zac thought. And the anticipation of seeing his expression when he caught sight of her all dolled up and wearing this dress was incentive enough to make her reach for it with gentle hands and slide it off the hanger.

Mavis smiled her approval as she unzipped it with fumbling fingers, stepped into it and turned around. 'Help me with this, please? I'm all thumbs, and the last thing I need is to ruin the zip on the one dress I like.'

As the metal teeth slid into place, she took a deep breath and glanced down, her eyes widening at her rather impressive newly created cleavage, courtesy of the in-built bustier. If that didn't make a statement, nothing would.

'Right, my girl, turn around. Let's have a look at you.'

When she turned, she caught sight of her reflection in the mirror behind Mavis a second after her friend's mouth formed a perfect *O*.

'You're beautiful!'

'Don't sound so surprised.'

Mavis reddened. 'I didn't mean it like that. It's just I've never seen you look—I mean, you don't usually wear— Uh—'

'It's okay.' She patted Mavis's arm. 'I'm not a clothes horse—never have been—and I never wear make-up because I can't be bothered.'

Mavis puffed up, nodding emphatically. 'Well, you're lovely without it.'

Lana stepped closer to the mirror, turning her head side to side. 'Though I have to admit you've worked a minor miracle.'

The glittering moss-green eyeshadow and dark khol elongated her eyes to exotic proportions, the foundation created the illusion of perfect skin, and the whisk of bronzing powder gave her razor-sharp cheekbones a healthy glow. As for her lips, she'd gone for a neutral nude pink. Nothing too over the top, considering whatever colour she wore wouldn't last long if she had any say in it...

'The make-up has only enhanced what the good Lord gave you.' Mavis held out a pair of shoes. 'Now, put these on and let's get going, before us Cinderellas turn into pumpkins before the night has begun.'

Lana laughed at the mixed metaphor and slipped on a pair of Beth's fabulous sky-high stilettos in a matching jade, took a final look in the mirror and did a little twirl for good measure.

The emerald shot-silk sheath fitted her like a second skin, the rich colour bringing out the green flecks in her eyes, and for a girl who'd never felt beautiful in her life, nothing came close to describing how she felt right at that moment.

'You're going to knock his socks off, my girl. Just you wait and see.'

It wasn't just his socks she wanted to knock off, but Lana wisely kept that gem to herself—though by Mavis's knowing look, she'd read her coy smile pretty well.

In this dress she was a woman with grit and determination; a woman ready to show her man how far she was willing to go; a woman with more than flirting on her mind; a woman willing to take a chance on an incredible man.

'Ready?'

Mavis held out a clutch bag and Lana smiled her thanks, slipping the sparkly bag into her hand, straightening her shoulders and following her out through the door, knowing she was as ready as she'd ever be.

Lana hovered near the entrance to the ballroom, watching the women in their designer dresses beguile their dates, sip champagne and laugh, clearly without a care in the world.

She wanted to be like that: sophisticated and flirtatious and carefree, the type of woman a guy like Zac would want in his life hopefully for more than just a couple of weeks.

But she wouldn't think about that now. Tonight was about showing him she wanted him as much as he wanted her. Tonight was a night for romance, for magic, for a shy girl to spread her metaphorical wings, preen and fluff out her feathers, demonstrate there was more to her than shapeless dresses and baggy shorts.

With her heart beating in rhythm with the jazz ballad playing softly in the background, she took a deep breath, squared her shoulders and entered the ballroom.

Her fingers convulsed around her clutch the exact moment Zac caught sight of her.

He was deep in conversation with another officer when he glanced up and stopped, shock etched across his handsome face, before he mumbled something and strode towards her. His gob-smacked expression was vindication that her make-over had made a statement—though, by the reproof shadowing those cobalt blue depths, definitely not the kind of statement she'd wanted.

When he reached her he stopped dead, his greedy gaze roaming over her before reproach, even censure, crept into his steely eyes. 'What's all this?'

At that precise moment her world crumbled.

She'd imagined this magical moment all day, had built it up in her head to be picture-perfect, with Zac taking her hand, twirling her at arm's length, before pulling her close and whispering how incredible she looked.

She'd imagined he'd take one look at her dress, her hair, her make-up, and know she'd done all this for him, to drive him mad with lust, to prove she felt the same way.

She'd imagined him so crazy for her he wouldn't be able to keep his hands off her, to the point where he'd drag her out of the party and straight to his cabin, where she'd finally shrug off the last of her insecurities and show him what a little confidence did for a woman.

Never in her wildest dreams—or nightmares—had she

imagined the cutting criticism underlying his question, or the disapproval creasing his brow.

While her first instinct was to hitch up her skirt and flee, she wouldn't give him the satisfaction of knowing how deeply he'd hurt her, how she'd trusted him enough to do this and how he'd rejected her anyway.

'By *this* you mean the dress?'

His frown intensified as he glanced at her hair, her face. 'And the rest.'

She bit down on the inside of her lip so hard she drew blood. The pain of his disparagement was slicing her heart in two.

Drawing on the last of her inner resolve, she concentrated on keeping her tone flat, unemotional. 'The invitation said formal, so I made an effort.'

'I see.'

Like hell he did.

For all his cheap words about getting to know her, admiring her intelligence and the real her, he didn't have a clue.

She had to get out of here—had to leave before her humiliation was complete and she broke down. 'You know something? I don't think you do.'

His eyes narrowed, the electrifying blue brought into sharp focus. With his midnight curls slicked back, and a tux accentuating his broad shoulders, he was breathtakingly handsome—a rakish pirate who'd stolen her heart and plundered her emotions without thought or feeling.

She didn't wait for a response before she rushed out of the room, her head swivelling both ways before she made a dash for the heavy glass door leading to the main deck.

She ran as fast as three-inch stilettos would allow, ignoring the heavy footsteps racing after her and the wind whipping her dress against her legs as her feet flew across the deck.

She reached the main deck as he shouted, 'Lana—wait.'

As if. She reached a dead end, swivelled to the right—and her heel jammed. She pitched forward.

Before she could hit the deck he'd caught her, his saving grip an instant reminder of how all this had started. Considering how it was about to end, she would have been better off sprawling on her butt that first day.

'You're making a habit of this.'

Stiffening, she silently cursed her clumsiness, straightened instantly, and was irrationally disappointed when he released her. 'Was there something you wanted?'

You, she wanted this seafaring charmer to say. As if that would happen, after his reaction to her make-over.

'Why did you leave in such a hurry?'

Her disbelieving look could have created an iceberg. 'Why do you think?'

Her clipped response didn't alter his guarded expression. This was a waste of time, and the sooner she made it to the sanctity of her cabin, ripped off this dress and slipped into her comfy cotton PJs, the happier she'd be.

He dragged a hand through his hair, muttered an expletive. 'I've made a mess of this.'

Too right. And while every self-preservation mechanism told her to make a run for it *now,* she couldn't help but wonder why he'd reacted that way.

'What's going on? I knew there was something wrong the second you saw me.'

His remorseful grimace didn't quell the rolling, rollicking waves swelling in her belly, making her nauseous when the three-metre swells buffeting the ship didn't.

'I overreacted. Your transformation took me by surprise.'

Glancing down at her dress, remembering the shock of seeing her expertly made-up face in the mirror after Mavis had worked her magic, she shook her head. 'There has to be more to it.'

'There isn't.'

He shrugged, his shoulders impossibly broad in the tux he wore as well as he did his uniform. 'Don't you get it? I *like* the fact you don't go for all the artificial stuff most women do.'

'You mean I'm a plain Jane?'

Ironic—she'd never felt so beautiful, so transformed, and he preferred simple old Lana.

Tipping up her chin, he searched her face. For…what? Proof his opinion mattered to her? A telltale sign that what he said had cut deep?

Whatever he was looking for, he wouldn't find it. She'd become an expert at hiding her feelings from a young age—had fooled her dad into believing she didn't care about his string of women, had convinced Beth she was happy being a frumpy nerd, when in fact she longed to be as gorgeous and confident and outgoing as her cousin.

'I mean I prefer the real you—the woman who captured my attention the first second she fell at my feet.'

'Oh, really?' Her mouth twitched at the memory of their first meeting.

"Yes, really." He trailed a finger down her cheek—soft, sensitive. 'So what's with the war paint?'

'Don't you know?'

Surely her dramatic eyes, her shaded cheeks and her pearly pink lips along with the sexy dress were enough of a clue?

Confusion creased his brow. 'Know what?'

'I did all this for *you*.' She gestured towards her dress,

her hair, her face. 'To show you there's more to me than just a brain and a smart mouth.'

His frown deepened. 'But I already know there's more to you. You're a gym instructor, for starters.'

She had to tell him. All of it. Now that she'd fallen for him, hoped for a future with him, he had to know.

Besides, it wasn't as if she'd deliberately lied to him. She'd just let him assume she was a boppy, trendy fitness freak, rather than a boring, conservative curator.

'Actually, I'm not a gym instructor.'

'What do you mean?'

'I don't work at a gym. I'm just a member.'

His jaw clenched. 'Then where *do* you work?'

'At the Sydney Museum. I'm head curator there.'

His muttered expletive had her repressing a smile.

'Tell me you're a qualified aerobics instructor and I haven't hired someone liable to send my insurance premiums to the bottom of the ocean?'

'Don't worry. I'm qualified. It's a hobby.'

He shook his head, as if trying to fathom what sort of a crazy person would work in a museum all day, then become a gym instructor for kicks.

Propping her elbows on the railing, she leaned back. This might take a while, and when she'd bored him senseless he'd probably jump overboard.

'I'll give you the abbreviated version. I was raised in Melbourne. You know about my botched relationship. When it soured, I moved to Sydney. Not just because of Jax, but to get away from myself, start afresh. I wanted to try new things, do stuff outside my comfort zone, so I joined a gym.'

She'd never forget her first step class, when she'd slunk in wearing a faded T-shirt and baggy tracksuit pants and been confronted by twenty Lycra-clad fitness fanatics in fancy joggers.

'I made a sloth look good, so joining a gym was huge for me. The bizarre thing was I got hooked to the point where I took an instructor's course. Not that I'll ever do anything with it—' he raised an eyebrow '—after this cruise, that is. But it was something I needed to do—something to build my confidence, to chalk up in my quest to try new things.'

Something shifted in his eyes. Wariness? Hurt? She belatedly realised he'd probably add himself to that list.

'Curator, huh?'

'Yeah.' She flicked her hair over her shoulder, not used to wearing it softly curled with tendrils tickling her.

'I guess it fits.'

His eyes hadn't lost their brooding expression, and her heart sank further. She'd hoped that by telling him the truth he might soften a little, understand where she was coming from. By the look of his compressed mouth and the deep groove between his brows he didn't.

'Fits?'

'Your image…before this.'

He waved towards her in a vague gesture, and acute disillusionment made her want to rip the designer dress off and fling it overboard.

'Before looking like a woman who wants to impress a man?'

He shook his head, thrust his hands into his pockets. 'You don't need to go in for all this fake stuff to impress me.'

'But you said—' She bit her tongue, wishing she had more experience with men, wishing she had half a clue where to go from here.

She'd tried to show him she wanted him by changing her appearance but he didn't get it. Worse—he didn't like it.

So what was her next move? Tell him outright? Yeah, like she'd have the guts to do that.

'What did I say?'

'Nothing, Popeye.'

'Popeye?'

At last she'd made him smile—albeit by a slip of the tongue.

She held up her hand. 'Don't you dare make a wisecrack about your muscles!'

She expected him to laugh, but instead he held her gaze a moment longer, his eyes gleaming with desire before it faded as fast as his smile.

Shaking his head, he raked a hand through his hair. 'I'm sorry, but I really have to go. We've got a PR disaster in the making on our hands, and I need to deal with it.'

'And?'

There was more: she could see it in the clenched jaw, the rigid shoulders.

'Add to that the fact my work schedule triples in the final two days of a cruise.'

He was dumping her, in no uncertain terms, before they'd even properly started.

She hadn't expected this, couldn't have braced herself for it, seeing how he'd been acting towards her before tonight, and nothing could stop the sharp, stabbing pain cleaving her in two.

Mustering the limited reserve that had got her through the confrontation with her CEO when he'd told her she wasn't 'assertive' enough to go on the Egypt jaunt, she effectively blanked her expression.

'I understand.'

He reached out to her, but her infinitesimal move back had him dropping his hand uselessly to his side. 'It's business.'

'Business. Right.'

The first prickle behind her eyes had her frantically searching for the nearest escape. She couldn't cry, wouldn't cry, and she'd be damned if she showed him he had the power to make her do so.

'You better get to it, then.'

She turned on her heel and walked away, head held high, though her impulse was to hike up her skirt and make a run for the welcome seclusion of her cabin.

This was what happened when she stepped out of her comfort zone, when she tried to be someone she wasn't: an awful, unmitigated disaster that would take her a lifetime to recover from.

She'd tried to make a big statement. Well, she'd done that all right. Pity Zac wasn't interested in reading the signs or hearing what she had to say or anything else.

She bit her top lip to stop the sobs bubbling up from deep inside. She hated the taste of the lipstick, wishing she could swipe a forearm across her mouth and wipe it off. But she was already drawing curious glances from the odd passer-by strolling on deck, and she had a reputation to uphold even though her instructor contract would be fulfilled tomorrow.

Even here, now, she couldn't shrug off her responsible work ethic, and at the thought of returning to the museum next week, with sadness in her heart and no charming smiles from a suave sailor to brighten her days, a lone tear seeped from the corner of her eye and ran down her cheek.

Picking up the pace, she ran for her cabin, wishing she could run from the mess she'd made with Zac as easily.

Zac clenched his fists and shoved them deep into his pockets, torn between wanting to chase after Lana and jumping overboard.

Both options held the same danger: he'd be floundering way over his head.

He'd deliberately driven her away.

He'd seen the hurt in her eyes, in the tremble of her lip, and he'd felt lower than pond scum. But what choice did he have?

He'd planned on telling her the truth tonight, about exploring their relationship further after this cruise, but he couldn't do it now. Her little bombshell had put paid to that.

As if the dramatic change in her appearance hadn't already set him on his guard, the truth behind her move to Sydney sealed it.

She was a woman seeking change, a woman dissatisfied with her current life, a woman searching for something new.

A woman like Magda.

He'd survived losing Magda, had lived through the pain of seeing her change before his very eyes, had hidden the devastation when she'd walked out on him in search of more than he could give.

It had taken him years to figure out they never would have worked, even if he hadn't gone back to shipping. Magda had been needy, demanding all his attention, wanting to be the focus of his world. Their initial attraction had been powerful, all-consuming, and he'd mistaken it for love. He had given up his career for her temporarily, would have done anything she asked in those heady honeymoon months.

But his folly had cost him dearly—had nearly killed his uncle. Which was exactly why he couldn't let him down now.

Though maybe he was being a tad harsh? Lana was nothing like Magda. She didn't demand to be noticed; in fact the opposite. It had been her lack of artifice that had first drawn him to her; her natural vivacity had been a refreshing change.

Everything in his life was fake, all about 'show' for the passengers, yet she was real—so real he could hardly believe it. He felt good when he was with her, felt as if his life wasn't a sham, especially with the current subterfuge driving him to distraction.

He wanted to feel that good all the time. Wanted to cement their relationship and take it as far as it could possibly go.

And he'd just learned she had a fulfilling career of her own—a job that would need her attention during those long months when he wasn't around if he took a chance on a long-distance relationship.

But should he? After tonight's metamorphosis, after what he'd learned, he'd be a fool ten times over to contemplate taking their relationship further. She was hell-bent on trying new things, on boosting her confidence. What if he was just part of her quest?

She'd seemed so natural, so unaffected, so real. But did he really know her at all?

Unexpected pain, deep and raw, gnawed his gut at the thought of not seeing her every day, not hearing her quick comebacks or her gentle teasing.

He'd grown to love the way her eyes lit up when she saw him, the way her lips curled up at the corners when she was thinking, the way she blushed when his teasing hit too close to the mark.

Grown to love?

Hell, no! He couldn't love her.

He wanted to test the waters with her, see if they could have a long-distance relationship without the complications of love and need and expectation.

Love complicated everything. Love tugged at his loyalties, making him choose between an uncle he couldn't abandon and a woman who'd stolen his heart without trying.

But what if it was too late?

He loved her.

And he'd hurt the woman he loved. He hated what he'd done to her tonight, all in an act of self-preservation.

She was too special. She didn't deserve to be treated that way. He needed to make amends.

Starting tomorrow, when he'd wrestled this irrepressible, overwhelming, surprising emotion into some semblance of control.

CHAPTER ELEVEN

WHEN the ship docked at Vila the next morning, Lana almost bolted down the gangway. Anything to escape a possible encounter with the man she could happily strangle with her bare hands.

She'd pegged him for a smart guy. Well, he couldn't be too smart if he hadn't read the signs last night—the biggest, most glaring sign of all being her dressed to the hilt.

Not that she'd be wearing that dress again. It now lay in a rumpled, crushed heap on the floor of her cabin, after she'd ripped it off and flung it into the corner the minute she'd got back last night.

She felt like her old self today—well, almost, if she discounted a broken heart—in long baggy cut-offs, a loose tank top and comfy leather sandals.

As for trying to get enigmatic sailors to believe she was willing to put her heart on the line for them—never again.

She planned on having Room Service for the last dinner tonight, and on skulking from deck to deck to avoid Zac. Irrational, as he could easily find her by waiting outside the gym at the end of her aerobics classes, but she'd face that particular scenario if and when it happened.

Though after last night she seriously doubted he'd be seeking her out again. He'd made that more than clear.

Touring Vila, the lovely capital of Vanuatu, proved to be a good distraction for a few hours, but once she reboarded the jitters started again, and she slunk from the staircase to her cabin, darting quick glances up the corridors in the hope of avoiding him. She needed to get past this—get a grip.

With a muttered curse that rarely slipped past her lips, she fumbled her key before jamming it in the lock.

'I thought I'd find you here eventually.'

She jumped, her heart sinking as Zac's deep voice rippled over her, still holding the power to set her pulse racing.

Determined to play it cool, she turned. 'Was there something you wanted?'

'You know damn well what I want.'

He had the audacity to try a roguish smile after what had happened last night?

Her eyes narrowed as she tried her best death glare—the one that got co-workers to do her bidding without a word.

'Actually, I don't. I have no idea what's going on in that big head of yours.'

'Big head? Now, that's the woman I know and love.'

Her heart skipped a beat, several beats, before she realised it was a figure of speech.

'I'm tired.'

His smile faded when he reached for her hand and she snatched it away. 'We need to talk.'

'I don't think so. You made it pretty clear how you feel last night.'

'That's what I want to talk about.' He rubbed the back of his neck as if he had a pain there; probably her. 'All I'm asking for is a chance to explain.'

She should send him on his way. She should ignore the

tiny flicker of hope kindling deep inside. Instead, her stance softened under the hint of vulnerability in his eyes, at his earnest, almost pleading expression.

She held up a finger. 'You get one chance.'

His ecstatic grin had the corners of her mouth twitching in response. 'I finally figured it out.'

'What?'

'What you were trying to show me last night.'

She bit back the words *about bloody time*. The confidence her make-over had inspired was a crumpled heap, along with the dress. She couldn't have this conversation now—not in the corridor outside her cabin. She could invite him in… A thought she contemplated for all of two seconds before discarding it as quickly as her make-up last night.

'When I told you how much I wanted you the other night I said I'd back off until you showed me you wanted me as much.'

Her skin started prickling as she shuffled from foot to foot. She *soooo* didn't want to talk about this now, but with his intense gaze fixed on her she had nowhere to hide.

Reaching out, he touched her cheek softly, a brief, tender touch that conveyed more than words ever could. 'I think you were trying to show me last night, but I was too hung up on irrelevant things to really notice.'

His eyes searched hers for confirmation, and all she could do was stand there like a dummy, racking her brain for a quick comeback, a brush-off, anything coherent, and coming up empty.

Leaning forward, he brushed her ear with his lips. 'I'm as emotionally involved in all this as you are. Maybe more. And I want to show you how much.'

His warm breath fanning her neck sent a shudder of

yearning through her. His declaration left her in little doubt what he meant.

Heck, she'd always thought actions spoke louder than words, and if they'd made a mess of things trying to articulate how they felt maybe she should go for broke and let him *show* her?

Taking a deep breath, and hoping her voice wouldn't quiver as much as her insides were at that moment, she said, 'Last night was a big deal for me. I was trying to make a statement, to show you I'm not just some mousy geek.'

His hand rested on her hip, caressed her, gently tugged her closer. His molten gaze, an incandescent blue like the hottest flame in a fire, was riveted to her lips.

'Mousy geek? More like sex goddess.' He dipped his head, stole a kiss, tempting her, confusing her. 'And you want to know what else I think?'

He cradled her chin, tipped it up so she had no option but to meet his blazing gaze head-on.

'I think you hide behind those old clothes of yours when inside is a passionate, exciting woman struggling to break free. A woman wanting to express herself. A woman who is driving me crazy with how much I want her.'

With her heart thundering in her chest, filling her ears with its pounding, she could pretend it had drowned out his words. But it hadn't. She'd heard every single word. All of them true.

She *did* want to break free, to express the passion bubbling away beneath the surface, locked away where no man had untapped it.

Here was a man who could do it, a man who'd captured her imagination closely followed by her heart from the first moment she'd met him, despite all protests to the contrary.

Here was a man who could give her what she'd craved since his first scintillating kiss: fulfillment.

Mustering every ounce of courage she possessed, she stepped into his personal space. 'My showing you last night didn't work quite as I intended, so how about I show you like this?'

She stood on tiptoe, brushed her lips against his, initiating a kiss for the first time in her life. And it felt great. Liberating. Incredible.

Zac moaned and grabbed her hand. 'Come with me.'

She clung to his hand, almost tripping in her haste to keep up with his long strides as they followed several staircases marked 'CREW ONLY'.

Wouldn't Beth have a field-day with this? Her conservative cousin being dragged off to a sailor's cabin! Oh, yeah, there'd be at least a year's worth of gossip out of this!

She muffled a snort and he slowed. 'Going too fast for you?'

'It's taken us this long to get to this point. What do you think?'

His answering grin held wicked promises she intended on holding him to as he picked up the pace, guiding her through a host of warren-like corridors before stopping in front of D21 and inserting a key.

'I know we could've used your cabin, but this way you have the option of leaving any time you like,' he said, stepping aside to let her in. 'Because if it'd been the other way around I wouldn't leave your side till you booted me out the door.'

Her heart soared, and she wondered how she could have ever doubted him? To understand her enough to know this was a big deal, to know she might want to flee to the privacy of her cabin later if things got too much—simply, he was incredible.

Reality hit as she entered the tiny cabin and her gaze riveted on the bed. She and Zac were about to make love—unreserved, unashamed, undeniably hot, sizzling, exhilarating love.

He paced the confined space like a caged leopard, raking a hand through his hair and looking just as dangerous.

'Zac?'

He swivelled towards her, his expression torn while his hungry gaze roamed her body. 'You're sure about this?'

Heck no!

What if she was lousy in bed? Frigid, just like Jax had said? What if she disappointed him? Or, worse, what if they were cataclysmically brilliant together and she fell further for him?

She fiddled with the neckline of her top, surprised by the flicker of irrepressible desire in the glittering blue depths of his eyes. If this daggy old top turned him on, he really must like her.

'Nothing in life is a surety. We've got tonight. Let's not waste it.'

His lips curved into a deliciously dangerous smile as he held a hand out to her. 'Didn't anyone ever warn you about sailors?'

Showing more bravado than she felt now the moment of truth had arrived, she placed her hand in his. 'Oh, yeah. Luckily I gave up listening a long time ago.'

He tugged gently on her hand till she stood less than a foot away. 'You're one hell of a woman.' He traced a line along her jaw, tilting her chin upwards. 'And I intend to make this a night we'll never forget.'

Her heart slammed against her ribs and her pulse tripped in anticipation.

'Show me.'

Their gazes locked, the wild yearning in his sending a jolt of answering desire through her body.

Her breasts tingled, her stomach dropped and her knees quivered as he stepped away, his stare bold, assessing, as it raked her body, strongly seductive yet soft as a caress.

'Let me look at you.'

Her breath hitched as he tugged her top over her head and dispensed with her bra with a deft flick. His sure hands making light work of the side zip on her pants too.

'I feel naked,' she breathed on a sigh, as his fingertips skated around her knickers—practical white cotton, unfortunately. Being seduced by the man of her dreams had been the last thing she'd expected today. He toyed with the elastic, making excitement ripple through her.

'Almost…'

His sizzling glance from beneath lowered lids sent her self-consciousness about her plain panties evaporating, along with the last of her nerves.

Zac wanted her. *Her.* All of her—her comfy clothes, boring knickers and quick brain—and she'd never felt so special. If she'd needed a confidence boost, the adoration in his eyes as he scanned her body was it.

The air whooshed out of her lungs as he kissed his way down her body, slow, soft kisses trailing a path to her abdomen and lower, where she throbbed with uncharacteristic fervour.

She'd never felt remotely like this, had barely registered much pleasure at all during sex with Jax, yet Zac's lips, followed by his fingertips skating across her skin with infinite precision, had her wanting to fist her hands in his hair and shove him where she burned the most.

'Ooh…'

Her pelvis bucked as he slipped one finger, another, under the elastic of her panties, caressing her folds, teasing her, pleasing her with a few simple strokes.

'May I?'

He raised his head and she nodded, biting on her bottom lip to stop from crying out with the pleasure of it all.

With torturous patience he peeled her panties down, his hands stroking her legs all the way to her toes while easing her back onto the bed.

She squeezed her eyes shut against the sight of herself lying open for him, naked, and tried to ignore the inevitable doubts that accompanied being this exposed.

She didn't have a supermodel body, or big breasts, or long legs. Instead she had a hint of cellulite on the tops of her thighs and breasts that wouldn't win any wet T-shirt competitions.

She'd always felt inadequate naked, had never felt sexy, and Jax had reinforced her insecurities.

'You're beautiful.'

At that moment, with his gaze travelling over her, drinking in every flawed detail before looking her in the eyes with reverence in his, she almost believed him.

Her breath caught as he grazed her clitoris, once, twice, and she almost came before he lowered his head again.

She tensed as his hot breath fanned her. Her hand stilled him.

'I've never done this before.'

His head snapped up. His shocked expression would almost have been comical if she didn't feel such a novice.

'What I mean is I've had sex, but—not this.'

She waved towards her nether regions, heat flushing her cheeks as a gratified glint turned his eyes electric blue.

'Then I'm proud to be your first.'

With the first sweep of his tongue any lingering resistance evaporated.

With the second she clenched her hands to stop herself from digging them into his shoulders to hold him down.

With the third her thighs fell open all the way, and her eyes drifted shut as she savoured the mind-blowing sensation sparking through her body.

This was all too much, yet too little, as he kissed her intimately, swirling his tongue, nibbling, varying the pressure and the rhythm till she exploded on a loud cry, sobbing with the sheer, mindless rush of it all.

'Hell, are you okay?'

He wiped her tears away with the pad of his thumb, so gently, so tenderly, she wept harder.

'Lana, talk to me.'

As he cradled her close she clung to him, burying her face in his chest, where her tears quickly gave way to chuckles.

He stilled. 'Are you laughing or crying?'

'Both,' she mumbled, inhaling, savouring the addictive scent of sea air and Zac imprinted on his skin.

He pulled away and stared down at her in confusion. 'You know, those are two reactions guaranteed to make a guy feel mighty insecure after what just happened.'

She reached up and cradled his cheek. 'Sorry, I'm just overwhelmed.'

How could she articulate what she felt? The gift he'd just given her?

He covered her hand with his and planted a soft kiss on her mouth. 'You don't have to say anything.'

Smiling, she turned her hand over, intertwined her fingers with his, hoping he could read half of what she was feeling in her eyes.

'I want to… What you just did for me…'

'My pleasure.'

His wicked grin made her laugh, defusing the tension and giving her the courage she needed to tell him the rest.

'I'm guessing by my reaction to you that I'm not frigid?'

He swore and squeezed her hand. 'Who told you that?'

'My ex. The only guy I've ever had sex with.'

Realisation dawned, and his expression was thunderous. 'So not only is the jerk lousy in bed, he blames his partner? Nice.'

'I always thought the problem was me.'

So the old adage of sailors swearing was true, she thought, as the expletives tripping from his tongue at a rate of knots made her blush.

He cupped her face and stared into her eyes—direct, compelling.

'Listen to me. You're a vibrant, responsive woman and you drive me crazy. Promise me you'll forget everything that jerk said.'

She wanted to believe him, she really did, but how did he know, considering they hadn't technically had sex?

'But we haven't—you know—done anything.'

His lips curved into a delicious smile, a smile of promise. 'The way you just responded to me, sweetheart, we've done enough.'

No, they hadn't. If he made her feel this good with his mouth, imagine how exciting the rest would be.

Trying a coy smile, she met his darkened gaze. 'I want you.'

His eyes burned, hot and hungry, and his answering smile was pure devilry. 'The feeling's mutual.'

More emboldened than she'd ever thought possible, she slipped a hand between them, stroking his erection through his trousers, enjoying the shocked widening of his eyes.

Stilling her hand, he said, 'We'll take things slow.'

She didn't want slow. Slow would give her time to think and analyse, let a few of those old insecurities creep up. She didn't want to think—not now. She wanted to feel and savour and enjoy.

'Actually, I'm thinking fast.'

She blushed at her audacity, her nipples hardening as she leaned forward and rubbed against the crisp cotton of his shirt, desperate to feel skin on skin, to feel all of him.

'We'll go slow later.'

'Whatever you want.'

Her fingers were frantic as they fumbled buttons, tripped over ties and snagged on zips, but the end result—a gloriously semi-naked Zac—was well worth it.

Her bravado halted at his tight black boxers, her fingers trembling.

'Here. Let me.'

He shucked them, and her eyes widened.

'Can I touch you?'

He nodded, his beautiful blue eyes heavy-lidded with passion, his gaze smouldering.

Her hand shook as she enclosed him, hard velvet pulsing in her palm. She stroked him to the tip and back, easing down and up again, empowered, emboldened, decidedly wanton.

'You're driving me crazy.'

His voice cracked and, high on her newfound sexual power, she knelt before him, eager to taste him, to give him half the pleasure he'd given her.

Before she could take him in her mouth he dropped to his knees and reached for her.

'As much as I appreciate the sentiment, I want you so badly I'm not going to last five seconds if you do that.'

She raised an eyebrow, delighting in his tortured expression as her tongue flicked out to moisten her bottom lip and his gaze riveted to it.

'Do what?'

With a growl, he swept her into his arms and tumbled her onto the bed, where her laughter quickly petered out as he lay beside her, the heat of his body igniting hers as he cradled her head and plundered her mouth.

Sensation rocketed through her as his tongue duelled with hers, firing her blood, her imagination, and everywhere in between.

She whimpered as his hand slipped between her legs, her body throbbing and eager and yearning for release as his fingers worked their magic.

'I want you inside me,' she gritted out as she arched into him, clutching at his shoulders as the tension within grew and expanded and finally detonated on a shattering explosion into ecstasy.

He slanted a searing kiss across her quivering lips. 'You can have me.'

She should have been thinking about protection, thinking about the consequences of not using any, but with her body humming, floating on a plane it had never reached once before, let alone twice, all logic had fled.

Thankfully he rolled a condom on before rolling her on top of him, and his gaze was adoring as he gently pushed her up into a sitting position till she straddled him.

'You're incredible.'

His hands skimmed her waist, drifting slowly upwards to cup her breasts, teasing her nipples with the barest brush of his thumbs, sending aftershocks through her.

The faintest of spasms shuddered through her. The tension was building again, coiling tighter and tighter, ready to send her into orbit this time.

She sucked in her breath as his hands spanned her hips, lifted her as he surged upwards, thrusting into her till she cried out.

'You okay?'

'Never been better.'

She clenched her internal muscles—her scarcely used internal muscles—to show him exactly how much better she was with him inside her, and was thrilled by the flicker of shock in those endless blue eyes.

'You wanted fast, right?'

He thrust into her again, harder, deeper, and she gasped, her thighs quivering as he spread her a tad more.

'Fast is good,' she managed to say, as he drove in again and again, each thrust sending her closer to the brink, each thrust a lesson in exquisite pleasure, each thrust showing her exactly how great sex could be with the right person.

Though this was more than sex, and she knew it.

But she wouldn't think about that now—wouldn't think beyond the earth-shattering spasms building, climbing, snaking their way through her pelvis and spreading outwards till she could barely feel anything beyond the torturously exquisite tremors rendering her mindless.

Finding a natural rhythm, she picked up the tempo, glorying in his ragged breathing, his glazed gaze, his straining muscles as he pushed them both towards a climax big enough to cause a tidal wave to swamp the ship.

'Jeez.'

She collapsed on top of him, stunned and sated and satisfied—very, very satisfied—savouring his strong arms as he cuddled her close.

'Lana?'

'Hmm?'

She snuggled deeper into his chest, knowing she could happily stay there for ever.

And now they'd made love and proved what she already knew—she'd fallen in love with him—well, things were about to get interesting.

He ran a finger down her bare arm, from shoulder to elbow, dipping briefly into the hollow before continuing to her wrist, where her pulse beat frantically.

'You're not frigid. And I intend to prove it. Over and over again. All night.'

She whimpered, a low, desperate, needy sound, and she clutched at his shoulders, hanging on as he flipped her onto her back and propped over her.

'What do you think about that?'

She smiled, slid her hands down his chest, savouring the rasp of hair against her palms. 'What are you waiting for?'

Zac didn't need to be asked twice.

He growled, nuzzled her neck, and smiled when she giggled, a pure, uninhibited sound of joy.

She was incredible. The sex he'd been fantasising about had far surpassed his wildest dreams. To think some stupid bastard had called her frigid, dented her self-esteem, kicked her confidence. Little wonder she'd used to look at him as if he was some kind of monster at times.

But not now.

Now she gazed at him from beneath half-lowered heavy lids, her molten caramel eyes glowing with satisfaction, the green flecks glittering with excitement. She wanted him as much as he wanted her, and he'd make damn sure he obliterated any last lingering doubts that she was anything other than pure sex goddess.

'I'm going to do this all night.'

Her breath caught as he licked a slow trail from the tip of her shoulder to her earlobe, where he lingered and nibbled.

She moaned, and he tensed. He'd never heard anything so sexy, and he could scarcely believe he'd only just had mind-blowing sex, considering his straining erection.

'Can I explore you?'

Her hesitant question had him wanting to sweep her into his arms and cradle her close. The hint of vulnerability beneath her soft tone was enough to fell the strongest man. Considering he'd already fallen for her, all she had to do was glance in his direction and he was all hers.

'Go ahead.'

Thrilled by her eagerness, he lay back and folded his hands behind his head, watching her.

Lust rocketed through him as she placed a soft, open-mouthed kiss on his neck, another one above his collarbone, before flicking her tongue out to lick him, a tentative flick that had him twitching.

He groaned as she nipped the sensitive areola, flicking a nipple with her tongue.

'Do you like that too?'

Her tongue traced lazy circles around it, and her voice held more than a hint of wonder at his response.

'Like it? You're driving me wild.'

She stopped, raised her head, and sent him a smile that could have tempted Neptune. 'Good.'

'Is that right?'

He surged upwards, his mouth seeking hers hungrily. Needing her more than she'd ever know.

Her head fell back and her lips parted on a whimper as his tongue plunged inside, teasing and stroking, almost ravishing her in a deep, devouring kiss, while his hands took on a life of their own, roaming and exploring her curves.

'You're so soft,' he murmured against her lips, praying he'd have the control to make this last all night, just as he'd promised.

For, come morning, he had another promise to discuss with her—one he hoped she'd go for in a big way.

He slid his palms up her ribcage to her breasts, feeling the nipples pebble as her heart thudded beneath his touch. He knew his own matched her beat, the rapid staccato rhythm sending blood pumping to every inch of his body. She moaned as he skimmed his palms repeatedly over her nipples and she arched up to meet him.

'Zac, you're killing me.'

He smiled, reached over the bedhead and grabbed a condom. 'Not yet—but the night is young.'

She smiled, gnawed on her bottom lip before holding out her hand.

'Here, let me do that.'

Surprised at her willingness to take care of the essentials, he handed it over, watched her rip the foil open and finger the rubber as if it was priceless parchment. For all her limited experience, she sure knew how to drive a man crazy. Sweat broke out across his upper lip as desperate need tore through him at her first tentative touch.

'How's that?'

She unrolled the rubber slowly, every minute movement a lesson in exquisite torture.

He groaned and stilled her hand, on the brink of losing control. Again. 'Perfect.'

'Good.'

She caressed his cheek, hooked a leg over his hip and rose to meet him in an erotic invitation he was powerless to refuse.

Sliding forward, he entered her inch by inch till they were locked tight. He'd never known such a feeling of completeness, of being totally one with another person, and if he'd had any doubts that a long-distance relationship was the way to go, the realisation she could be his soul-mate dispelled them in an instant.

But for now they had tonight and he intended to show her exactly how much she meant to him, how much he hoped for the future, by making love to her with every inch of his body.

'That feels amazing.'

She arched into him, torching his body, rousing it to fever-pitch as he pumped into her, his thrusts setting her breasts jiggling, his excitement ratcheting up to an unbearable level as he watched them.

She threw her head back and, listening to her soft, urgent moans, he knew she was close as with each practised stroke he took her to the brink.

He wanted to wait, to make it last, but with his own climax hovering she screamed out his name and bucked into him, sending him over the edge. Spasms ripped through him, a galaxy of shooting stars exploding in his head as he shot to the moon and back.

How had he ever fooled himself into believing this was just about a light flirtation at the beginning?

The connection he shared with this funny, smart, quirky woman was real, was unique, and was so damn perfect he'd be a fool to let her do anything but agree to his plans tomorrow.

'You're incredible.' He brushed a kiss across her lips as she snuggled closer, stunned by the ferocity of his love for her.

Damn, he needed space—a few minutes to reassemble his wits before he blurted his feelings in the heat of the moment and scared her.

'Just going to the bathroom for a sec, okay? Don't move an inch.'

Lana watched Zac, her gaze greedily roving his naked back, his butt, not in the least embarrassed.

After what had just happened, what they'd just shared, her insecurities had been well and truly blasted sky-high. But it was more than physical, more than cataclysmic sex and the exhilaration of being one.

Something had shifted between them.

She'd seen it in his eyes—a depth of caring that lifted her heart and transported her to a place of hope and dreams and beyond.

But she wouldn't dwell on emotions now. She had a whole night of snuggling in his arms to look forward to—and several repeat performances of the magic they conjured together.

Unable to wipe the self-satisfied grin from her face, she slipped out of bed to turn off the lamp on the desk, stubbing her toe on the way.

'Ouch!' She grabbed her foot and hopped around, stumbling against the desk and knocking a stack of papers to the floor.

Managing a wry smile—it looked as if her clumsy gene kicked in even when he wasn't around—she scooped up the papers, and several photos that had fallen out of an envelope.

Her heart stilled as she glanced at the photos. Every one depicted Zac: in front of Sydney's newest high-rise business centre in a designer suit, shaking hands with the Prime Minister, behind a huge conference table filled with international delegates, standing behind an older man with a hand on his shoulder and the name plaque 'CEO, Madigan Shipping' in front of him.

She stared at the photos, confused, a million questions buzzing through her brain.

Who *was* the guy she'd just made love to, had given her heart to?

He stepped out of the bathroom at that moment, a lazy grin on his face as he glanced towards the bed. His grin faltered as he looked towards the desk, at what she held in her hands, and the colour draining from his face.

'I guess you have some questions—'

'Who *are* you?'

She hated the uncertainty, the accusation in her voice. She shouldn't have pried, should have shoved the photos back where they belonged, but now she'd seen them she needed answers.

Running a hand through his mussed hair, he padded over to join her. 'I own this shipping company.'

'You *own* it?'

He nodded, managing to appear proud and bashful and ashamed all at the same time. 'I'm actually the new CEO of Madigan Shipping. My uncle used to run the company, but he recently handed over the reins to me. We haven't formally announced it yet.'

She didn't get this. Why would a CEO be working on one of the ships he ran?

'So what's the PR stint all about? Trying to keep a tight leash on your employees?'

'Nothing like that.'

He took a robe from a wardrobe hook and offered it to her. Mustering as much dignity as an indignant naked woman could, she shrugged into it like a queen into royal robes, grateful when he slipped his shirt and trousers back on. She could do without distraction while they had this cosy little chat, though by the sense of foreboding clawing its way to consciousness she knew they'd never be cosy again once they'd finished talking.

Indicating she take a seat, he perched on the edge of the bed. 'The company's being targeted by a saboteur. Small things at first—dangerous levels of chlorine in the pools, things we could catch before they did any real damage— but the incidents have been growing in severity. Now I need to find the culprit and put a stop to it.'

He paused, looking suitably shamefaced.

'To collect the evidence I need, I had to go undercover. This ship was the most likely to be attacked next, and no one knows who I am. As far as they know James Madigan is still CEO—a distant figurehead they'd never connect with me.'

She couldn't fault Zac for being dedicated to his job, for wanting to protect the company he owned. She of all people understood what it was like to be driven to be the best in her field. But if he didn't work on ships anymore, if he was now stuck behind that great big desk she'd glimpsed in the photos…

'Where are you based?'

The instant he looked away she knew.

He *wasn't* married to his precious job aboard ships.

He *wasn't* so enamoured of the sea he'd never leave it for her.

He wasn't interested in her, period.

At least not enough to have a real relationship beyond this—this fling, or whatever it was they'd had.

'Where?'

Her voice had risen, and his gaze locked on hers, regret mingling with apology in those endless blue depths.

'Sydney.'

'Right.'

'Look, Lana, I was going to tell you—'

'Save it.'

Turning her back on him, she slipped off the robe and yanked on her old clothes, lying in a sad heap on the floor. A bit like her pathetic dreams of happily-ever-after.

She stalked to the door without a backward glance—had her hand on the handle before he crossed the small space and slammed his palm on the door.

'You need to hear me out.'

Holding her breath, determined not to breathe in and let his heady scent, his proximity, undermine her resolve to walk out of here with what little dignity she had left, she turned to face him.

'Actually, I don't.'

He didn't budge. 'I didn't tell you because I'm not going to be based in Sydney for the next year.'

She wouldn't ask him where he was going—wouldn't give him the satisfaction of showing a small part of her was curious, a small part of her still cared.

'I'll be based in London.'

'How nice for you.'

Her sarcasm fell on deaf ears as he fixed her with that steady, unwavering stare. So what if he appeared honest now? She couldn't trust one word falling from his mouth. Not when he'd been lying to her the entire time.

She hated liars.

Jax had lied to her, had feigned interest in her to get the inside scoop on some precious artefacts he wanted to add to his private collection, had belittled her. He'd ruined what little self-confidence she'd ever had. But she hadn't really loved Jax as she loved Zac. So what the heck would she do this time around to cope with the devastation of being lied to by another rich guy playing games to suit his own ends?

He dragged his free hand through his hair, his expression crushed. 'My uncle's dying. He has a year to live, max. He's my only family and he's in London. I owe him. I have to be there for him.'

Her anger fractured. A tiny crack that allowed a modicum of sympathy to seep in.

But why was he telling her this? It was irrelevant. He'd still lied to her, had always known there'd be nothing between them beyond this fortnight.

'I was going to tell you. I was hoping we could try a long-distance relationship.'

Her tummy trembled as for one brief moment she contemplated what it would be like being involved with a guy like him for more than two weeks: to call him her boyfriend, to cross off days on a calendar, counting down the minutes till she saw the love of her life again.

But she couldn't do it.

If she couldn't trust him to tell her the truth when they were together, what hope would she have with him on the other side of the world for three hundred and sixty-five long, interminable days?

She needed honesty. She needed trust.

By his actions, Zac could give her neither.

With a shake of her head she placed a hand on his arm barring her escape and pushed.

'I'm not interested.'

She didn't have to push hard, as the second the words left her mouth an icy, impassive mask slid into place. His eyes were a cold, hard blue as his arm dropped and he stepped out of her way.

'Well, I guess I was just one of those new experiences you were so hell-bent on trying this trip.'

With soul-deep sadness clawing at her insides, robbing her of breath, she scrambled for the door handle.

'Hell. Lana, wait—'

She flung open the door so hard it almost fell off its hinges, then slammed it behind her and didn't look back.

CHAPTER TWELVE

ZAC sank onto the bed and dropped his head in his hands, the echo of the slamming door reverberating in his ears.

He'd stuffed up—made a major mess of things.

He should be hurt by Lana's refusal to contemplate a long-distance relationship, should be smarting.

But he wasn't. He knew the score.

He'd seen the devastation in her eyes when she'd learned the truth, and he knew it wouldn't have hurt that much if she didn't love him as much as he loved her.

Every one of her responses had been genuine, from the first moment he'd met her until now, so there was no mistaking the depth of feeling simmering below the surface, the raw pain he'd seen in her eyes.

He'd hated hurting her, however inadvertently, had wished he'd told her everything from the start. But it was too late for wishful thinking.

A part of him wanted to give her space, a year's worth of it, before coming back and trying again. He'd learned through his experience with Magda that if you loved someone enough you needed to give them space to grow and change. She hadn't wanted that space, but Lana would. She'd said as much in her quest for new things. Maybe he should give her a year to do what she had to do, then re-enter her life and start afresh?

As pain rocketed through him he knew he couldn't do it. He couldn't leave her that long. He loved her too much.

He was a man of action—prided himself on it. Business plans, mission statements, corporate policies—he could take a plan and turn it into reality. And that was exactly what he would do here.

He loved Lana, and he would prove it to her whatever it took.

And as much as he wanted to chase after her now, sweep her into his arms, cradle her close and tell her everything would be okay, he wasn't that stupid.

She needed time to calm down, time to evaluate, *really* evaluate what had happened here tonight. Before the photos, before the accusations, before the truth.

Simply, they were meant to be, and he had every intention of making that happen.

She'd been summoned to the bridge by the Captain for him to thank her for taking the classes. Great—just what she needed. Instead of disembarking as fast as she could, she'd have to go through the final rigmarole of playing the dutiful employee.

What a crock. This whole trip had been a crock, from start to finish, and she wished she'd never won the darn thing.

Knocking at the door, she grimaced at her reflection in the glass. Lucky things had ended with Zac last night, for if she'd been a plain Jane before and he'd still been attracted to her he'd swim a mile regardless if he saw the frightful mess she looked today.

Placing both hands against the glass, she peered into the massive room, glimpsed a flash of uniform on the other side.

All those gadgets probably made noise and had muffled her knock, so she opened the door, stepped into the huge control centre.

'Captain?'

She heard a footfall, sensed a presence behind her, and her skin prickled as if she'd eaten a crate of strawberries.

Oh-oh—a ship's captain she'd never met wouldn't have that effect on her. Only one man did. The same man she never wanted to see again as long as she lived.

'I needed to see you. The Captain was kind enough to do my dirty work.'

'That'd be right.'

Her voice quivered as she turned, faced him, hating the fact that after all the heartache the sight of him could still reduce her to this—a nervous wreck.

'I need to know if I've missed the boat.'

She stared at him as if he'd taken leave of his senses, glancing out of the huge windows at Circular Quay on her left, the Opera House on her right, and the ship firmly berthed at its moorings.

He gazed directly into her eyes. 'Have I?'

In an instant she knew he wasn't referring to the ship. 'What's this about?'

He tugged on his tie—totally skewed, she noticed. He didn't appear the consummate professional for once, with dark stubble covering his chin and bleary eyes surrounded by dark rings. He looked as bad as she felt.

'I've been going out of my mind since last night.'

She shrugged, unprepared for the swift stab of pain at the recollection of what they'd shared and lost last night. 'You should've thought of that before you lied to me.'

'Please, let me finish.'

He sounded like a little boy asking for the last toy boat

for his bathtub, and though her head told her to run, her heart told her to hold her ground.

'You shouldn't have discovered the truth by those photos. I—'

'It wasn't about the photos, damn it!'

She took a steadying breath, as surprised by her outburst as him. She never shouted or lost control. Well, not unless she counted the times when he'd made agonisingly sweet love to her last night.

He opened his mouth to respond and she held up a hand. 'It's the fact you're based in Sydney, the fact you're mega-rich, the fact we could've had more than two weeks if you hadn't let me believe—'

Let her believe he was a sailor. Let her believe his precious job was all-important. Let her believe for one, tiny speck in time she might actually mean more to him than a handy lay.

'Believe this.'

He swept her into his arms and kissed her—a divine, devastating kiss that demanded more than she was willing to give.

For all of two seconds.

Powerless to resist, she responded by softening her lips, allowing him access to her mouth. The logic of pushing him away was shattered by the hunger of his kiss.

Her eager response shocked her more than the kiss itself and she broke away, dragging in breaths to clear her fuzzy head.

'Damn it, I didn't mean for that to happen.'

He raked a hand through his hair, adding to his rumpled state, and she clenched her hands, shaken by how much she wanted to reach out and smooth it for him.

Shrugging, she wrapped her arms around her middle to ward him off. 'I guess it always came down to that for us, didn't it? A chemical reaction. Nothing more.'

'You're wrong.'

Grabbing hold of her arms, he left her no option but to look up—and what she glimpsed in his eyes sent a shiver of sorrow through her.

Pain. A soul laid bare. A soul lost and confused and reaching out. Just like hers.

'I didn't want to fall for you. I didn't want to get emotionally involved. But I did.'

'Just not enough?'

His declaration should have had her running outside, vaulting the rail and doing a perfect dive into the water, but it merely served to widen the gap. Too little, too late. She could never trust him now.

'It happened to me once before. In my early days while I was still working the ships. I fell for a passenger.' His mouth twisted into a grimace. 'I fell so hard I ended up marrying her.'

Shock speared her, and she tightened her arms around her belly to ward off the pain.

'I gave up my job for her—left the ships for a year. I gave the marriage everything, paid her the attention she demanded, but it wasn't enough. She couldn't handle my career when I went back to it, my absences. She changed. Her appearance, her outlook, her needs, her lover—'

Her gaze snapped to his. She was not surprised by the hard, unyielding blue, or the sadness underlying his bitterness.

'That's why I overreacted that night you had the makeover. Another woman I loved changing before my eyes. Stupid, I know.'

Her befuddled brain backed up a sentence or two, wondering if she'd heard him correctly.

He must have seen the confusion clouding her eyes, for he took advantage of her bewilderment by caressing her arms before his hands slid up to cradle her face.

'That's right. I love you. Whether you're a fitness instructor or a curator or dressed to the nines or in nothing at all. I love you.'

Her heart leapt at the sincerity in his voice, the tenderness in his eyes. She wanted to fling her reservations to the wind and leap into his arms.

But she couldn't. It looked as if her fortnight of being frivolous had ended when the ship docked, and now she was back in Sydney she couldn't shake her conservative ways.

'I appreciate you telling me. But what about the rest? Why didn't you come after me last night? Explain all this then?'

Instead she'd spent a sleepless night, alternating between cursing him, herself, and the great cosmos that had brought them together in the first place.

'Because I had to tie up loose ends.'

'Loose ends?'

Her heart sank. She *knew* his declaration of love was too good to be true.

'As you know, I'm the new CEO of Madigan Shipping. When I ditched my job for a year to be with Magda I didn't know my uncle was about to hand over the corporation to me. I let him down, and because of ongoing job stress he had a heart attack.'

She touched his arm, sorry for his genuine sadness.

'Uncle Jimmy raised me, funded my education. He has been like a father to me, and I owe him. And now he's dying…' He shrugged, pain pinching his mouth. 'I've discovered our saboteur. Turns out to be a disgruntled employee who we suspect may be mentally unstable. The authorities are waiting to take him into custody. But I still need to prove to my uncle I can do this—prove I'm trustworthy, prove I can make his legacy the best in the business, make this difficult time for him the least stressful as possible.'

'So you'll be based in London for a year?'

He nodded. 'I'm afraid that's the non-negotiable part of the deal.'

Perhaps her head still spun from his kiss and his declaration, because she didn't quite get what he was saying.

'What deal?'

He caressed her cheek, his hand slipping to cradle her head, his fingers winding deliciously through her hair. 'The deal where you and I give this relationship everything we've got, long-distance or not. The deal where you use your annual leave to board the company jet and come visit your desperate boyfriend. The deal where I spend a fortune on teleconferencing and e-mails and every other newfangled way on the planet to keep in contact with the woman I'm crazy about. The deal where you can try as many new things as you want as long as you don't forget about your boyfriend pining for you on the other side of the world.'

Gently angling her head, he slanted a slow, sensual kiss across her lips—a kiss that reached deep down and soothed the parts of her soul that had ached when she'd thought she'd lost him for good.

'That's the deal.'

He broke the kiss, rested his forehead against hers. 'And, being the incredibly successful magnate I am, I won't take no for an answer.'

'You have to know this trip wasn't just about trying new things for me. I needed to build my confidence, and thanks to you I have. But what if we try the long-distance thing and it doesn't work?'

She had to ask. Logic demanded it. But she was almost afraid of his answer as her heart dared to hope. If she took a chance on him, on them, and it didn't work, her confidence would take another dive, and she'd hate that after how far she'd come. Not to mention how she'd handle a shattered heart.

'It'll work. I won't settle for anything less.'

Her breath caught as he cradled her face, stared directly into her eyes.

'I love you. I'll always love you. All the oceans in the world can't keep us apart.'

Her heart expanded till she thought it would burst, and her legs joined her hands in the shaking stakes.

'I don't know what to say…' She blinked back tears as his thumb skated across her lips, grazed her cheek.

'I think you do.'

His lips brushed hers, slow, thoughtful, in a soul-reaching kiss that coaxed her into believing this was happening and this was real.

'I love you too,' she breathed on a sigh, clinging to him, powerless to do anything other than love this incredibly impressive man.

As he let out a jubilant whoop, louder than the ship's horn, she kissed him with all the passion, love and adoration she'd been storing away for days now—ever since she'd realised the terrifying truth: that she loved this man, would never love another as much as she loved him.

'I love you so much, sweetheart. Don't you ever run out on me again. Last night was the longest, loneliest night of my life.'

'Same here.' Snuggling into him, she breathed in his sinfully addictive scent, stunned she'd get to savour it for the rest of her life.

He nuzzled her neck and she squealed as he nipped her, his lips searing a trail towards her mouth as heat flooded her body, having a predictable response as she swayed towards him.

It had been like this right from the start. Her body had always known on some instinctual level that he was the man for her, while her head had taken a while to process the idea.

Zac loved her. This powerful, commanding, sexy guy loved her.

Life couldn't get any better.

'You know, I could always see if any of the London museums are interested in a top-notch curator on secondment.'

He pulled away, shock widening his eyes to endless blue proportions. 'You'd do that for me?'

'Only if you're good.'

With the same wicked smile he'd used to charm her from day one, he wrapped his arms around her, stroked her back, set her body ablaze.

'Oh, I'm better than good. I'm brilliant.'

'That's a pretty high recommendation to live up to, sailor boy.'

'Care to help me try?'

'Aye-aye,' she murmured, and his lips lowered to hers.

* * * * *

Turn the page for an exclusive extract from:
THE SHEIKH'S FORBIDDEN VIRGIN
by
Kate Hewitt

Taken by the sheikh for pleasure—but as his bride…?

At her coming-of-age at twenty-one, Kalila is pledged to marry the Calistan king. Scarred, sexy Sheikh Prince Aarif is sent to escort her, his brother's betrothed, to Calista. But when the willful virgin tries to escape, he has to catch her, and the desert heat leads to scorching desire—a desire that is forbidden!

Aarif claims Kalila's virginity—even though she can never be his! Once she comes to walk up the aisle on the day of her wedding, Kalila's heart is in her mouth: *who is waiting to become her husband at the altar?*

A LIGHT, INQUIRING KNOCK SOUNDED on the door, and, turning from that grim reminder, Aarif left the bathroom and went to fulfill his brother's bidding, and express his greetings to his bride.

The official led him to the double doors of the Throne Room; inside, an expectant hush fell like a curtain being dropped into place, or perhaps pulled up.

"Your Eminence," the official said in French, the national language of Zaraq, his voice low and unctuous, "may I present His Royal Highness, King Zakari."

Aarif choked; the sound was lost amid a ripple of murmurings from the palace staff, who had assembled for this honored occasion. It would take King Bahir only one glance to realize it was not the king who graced his Throne Room today, but rather the king's brother, a lowly prince.

Aarif felt a flash of rage—directed at himself. A mistake had been made in the correspondence, he supposed. He'd delegated the task to an aide when he should have written himself and explained that he would be coming rather than his brother.

Now he would have to explain the mishap in front of

company—all of Bahir's staff—and he feared the insult could be great.

"Your Eminence," he said, also speaking French, and moved into the long, narrow room with its frescoed ceilings and bare walls. He bowed, not out of obeisance but rather respect, and heard Bahir shift in his chair. "I fear my brother, His Royal Highness Zakari, was unable to attend to this glad errand, due to pressing royal business. I am honored to escort his bride, the princess Kalila, to Calista in his stead."

Bahir was silent, and, stifling a prickle of both alarm and irritation, Aarif rose. He was conscious of Bahir watching him, his skin smooth but his eyes shrewd, his mouth tightening with disappointment or displeasure, perhaps both.

Yet even before Bahir made a reply, even before the formalities had been dispensed with, Aarif found his gaze sliding, of its own accord, to the silent figure to Bahir's right.

It was his daughter, of course. Kalila. Aarif had a memory of a pretty, precocious child. He'd spoken a few words to her at the engagement party more than ten years ago now. Yet now the woman standing before him was lovely, although, he acknowledged wryly, he could see little of her.

Her head was bowed, her figure swathed in a kaftan, and yet, as if she felt the magnetic tug of his gaze, she lifted her head and her eyes met his.

It was all he could see of her, those eyes; they were almond-shaped, wide and dark, luxuriously fringed, a deep, clear golden brown. Every emotion could be seen in them, including the one that flickered there now as her gaze was drawn inexorably to his face, to his scar.

It was disgust Aarif thought he saw flare in their

golden depths, and as their gazes held and clashed he felt a sharp, answering stab of disappointment and self-loathing in his own gut.

* * * * *

Be sure to look for
THE SHEIKH'S FORBIDDEN VIRGIN
by Kate Hewitt,
available October from Harlequin Presents®!

HARLEQUIN *Presents*

TWO CROWNS, TWO ISLANDS, ONE LEGACY

A royal family torn apart by pride and its lust for power, reunited by purity and passion

THE ROYAL HOUSE *of* KAREDES

Look for the next passionate adventure in
The Royal House of Karedes:

THE SHEIKH'S FORBIDDEN VIRGIN
by Kate Hewitt, October 2009

THE GREEK BILLIONAIRE'S INNOCENT PRINCESS
by Chantelle Shaw, November 2009

THE FUTURE KING'S LOVE-CHILD
by Melanie Milburne, December 2009

RUTHLESS BOSS, ROYAL MISTRESS
by Natalie Anderson, January 2010

THE DESERT KING'S HOUSEKEEPER BRIDE
by Carol Marinelli, February 2010

HPI2859

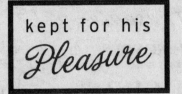

REQUEST YOUR
FREE BOOKS!

HARLEQUIN *Presents*

2 FREE NOVELS
PLUS 2
FREE GIFTS!

PASSION
GUARANTEED
SEDUCTION

YES! Please send me 2 FREE Harlequin Presents® novels and my 2 FREE gifts (gifts are worth about $10). After receiving them, if I don't wish to receive any more books, I can return the shipping statement marked "cancel." If I don't cancel, I will receive 6 brand-new novels every month and be billed just $4.05 per book in the U.S. or $4.74 per book in Canada. That's a savings of close to 15% off the cover price! It's quite a bargain! Shipping and handling is just 50¢ per book*. I understand that accepting the 2 free books and gifts places me under no obligation to buy anything. I can always return a shipment and cancel at any time. Even if I never buy another book, the two free books and gifts are mine to keep forever.

106 HDN EYRQ 306 HDN EYR2

Name	(PLEASE PRINT)	
Address		Apt. #
City	State/Prov.	Zip/Postal Code

Signature (if under 18, a parent or guardian must sign)

Mail to the **Harlequin Reader Service:**
IN U.S.A.: P.O. Box 1867, Buffalo, NY 14240-1867
IN CANADA: P.O. Box 609, Fort Erie, Ontario L2A 5X3

Not valid to current subscribers of Harlequin Presents books.

Are you a current subscriber of Harlequin Presents books and want to receive the larger-print edition? Call 1-800-873-8635 today!

* Terms and prices subject to change without notice. Prices do not include applicable taxes. Sales tax applicable in N.Y. Canadian residents will be charged applicable provincial taxes and GST. Offer not valid in Quebec. This offer is limited to one order per household. All orders subject to approval. Credit or debit balances in a customer's account(s) may be offset by any other outstanding balance owed by or to the customer. Please allow 4 to 6 weeks for delivery. Offer available while quantities last.

Your Privacy: Harlequin Books is committed to protecting your privacy. Our Privacy Policy is available online at www.eHarlequin.com or upon request from the Reader Service. From time to time we make our lists of customers available to reputable third parties who may have a product or service of interest to you. If you would prefer we not share your name and address, please check here. ☐

HP09R

EXTRA

DARK NIGHTS WITH A BILLIONAIRE

*Untamed, commanding—
and impossible to resist!*

Swarthy and scandalous, dark and dangerous, these
brooding billionaires are used to keeping women for as
many nights as they want, and then discarding them....

But when they meet someone who throws their best-laid
plans off track, will these imposing, irrepressible men
be brought to their knees by love?

**Catch all of the books in this fabulous
Presents Extra collection, available October 2009:**

The Venetian's Midnight Mistress #73
by CAROLE MORTIMER

Kept for Her Baby #74
by KATE WALKER

Proud Revenge, Passionate Wedlock #75
by JANETTE KENNY

Captive In the Millionaire's Castle #76
by LEE WILKINSON